I0582451

FATE & FORTUITY

SIGILIS SEPTERRA SHORT FANTASY COLLECTION 1

NIKI PATEL

BOUND SPINE PRESS

ISBN: 978-1-7364275-0-7 (ebook)

ISBN: 978-1-7364275-1-4 (paperback)

ISBN: 978-1-7364275-2-1 (hardcover)

ISBN: 978-1-7364275-3-8 (large print)

LCCN: 2022919685

Cover design by Maria Spada

Published by Bound Spine Press

South Brunswick, NJ

Content warning: While the stories in this book are enjoyable, there is mention of death by fire. Readers sensitive to this element please take note.

My grandfather,
I attempt to walk in your footsteps, but I find I have some big shoes to fill.

Contents

1

— . —

To Chase a Lore

T he antechamber echoed every footstep, every movement, especially when manacles and chains and stone floors were involved.

Guards fitted with breastplates and helmets stood stalwart beside
doors at both ends of the antechamber, their hands clutching halberds
as tall as them. With their eyes wary and muscles primed, they were ready
to leap into action at the slightest trouble, whether Overlord Drilll or his
guard commander gave any orders or not.

They expected silence, but I wasn't good at enforcing stillness. It taxed
my nerves and made me hot. And as each moment passed the baton of
apprehension to another, I itched to fidget. But that was not acceptable
either. However, nothing stopped me from stealing glances at the large
head of the fellow beside me and wondering how he balanced it atop his
slight frame.

Stealing? Yes, that was the reason for me being here.

The sharp spikes and the gleaming blades of the two-handed pole
weapons were threatening, and this part of the Manor was no less omi-
nous than the other, but I became distracted by the concern of the
weight-bearing capacity of the bench beneath us. It was narrow, forcing
our shoulders and arms to graze each other, and I was heavy, so it proved
its unsteadiness whenever I shifted my balance.

Being a vital component of Drilll's government, the guards were well
fed, and the fellow stinking of rank sweat beside me was not far off in

healthfulness from them. Still, if one were to borrow the measuring tape from Ashmere Manor's seamstress and make the effort of checking the girth of all men involved, I would win the contest. After all, I was the Manor's notable food taster.

Between glimpses at the men and the questionable bench, the tapestry opposite us—showcasing three ladies embroidering under fruit trees—served as a resting place for my eyes. The plump and ripe fruit, in particular, became a location of my focus. It helped to prevent my curiosity from getting me into a larger vat of trouble because prying citizens in Drilll's lands led an abbreviated life.

My existence was privileged, more than most inhabitants of Ashmere, more than Ephy, my wife, and Sonarus, my son, and far superior to when I'd reared pigs in my old village of Changewinds, in the southern part of the continent. But those days were gone. Drilll had menaced not just Changewinds but other villages on his way here from the neighboring continent of Terra Two. Countless towns and hamlets in this area were coerced and annexed into the ever-expanding city of Ashmere.

It had started with Drilll's father and a band of soldiers in the south. The success of clutching and exploiting his first town of Oldberg gave him such intoxicating pleasure that he went on expanding his army and seizing more and more lands. Soon Drilll followed his father's example and brought the terror to these mid-western parts. Terra Two's king, in turn, showered him with riches and extra soldiers.

A creak escaped into the air from beneath us. Both guards scowled in our direction, making me drag my attention to the ridges in the stones layering the floor, praying the bench remained intact until the governor called me into his chamber.

What if the bench cracked and crashed? Would the carpenter be reprimanded, too? How low did Drilll and the governor's tolerance go?

I slid my attention to my neighbor's shackled feet. His shoes had pointy toes . . . I had never come across such a design in Ashmere or in Changewinds. His clothes were different as well.

Most ordinary men of Terra One wore a buttonless, collarless shirt with a drawstring hem at the hips over long, loose trousers. In contrast, the man's attire was a droopy shirt with three buttons at the neck, tucked into trousers that ballooned at the top and narrowed toward the feet.

What was the reason for his presence here? And what was his destined punishment?

"Are you carrying any food?" the man whispered and startled me.

Now, that was something I would do: begin a conversation on the way to the butcher's block. Ephy chided me often for being foolish-brave, a valiant with a blindfold on, heedless to the onslaught of penalties lined up behind the deed that made my chest puff out more than usual.

He must have noted my surprise at the absurdity of the question since we were in a confined place deprived of liberty, but he continued, "I haven't eaten in six days, and you look like someone who would conceal food in his garments."

Shocked, I jerked my head at him, my eyebrows raised high. Then I remembered the guards. Creaking incident forgotten, they had returned to their posts and were still.

The prisoner crept his arms over and tugged at my drawstring. But how could I part with the stolen food, the very objects responsible for my capture? Besides, if, by some remote chance I escaped the encounter with the governor unharmed, my family could use it.

"Please!" The word was uttered so softly, the tail end of it was lost in the space between us. Except the urgency in his tone was not, and neither was the apparent pain of hunger. He was daring to ask for food in an area of imminent doom. It had to count for something.

He pulled on the loops of my string.

My hands flew to my middle in response, and the clamor from the chains linked to my shackles filled the narrow room. The tapestries adorning the walls couldn't keep the sound from rebounding.

Two rolls of bread, cheese, and a slice of mutton tumbling to the floor would condemn me to what the cook would call "the charred-crumbs-stuck-to-the-bottom-of-the-pot treatment"—the worst of the worst.

Both guards were upon us, the spear ends of their halberds at our necks.

I swallowed the lump in my throat, glad I had pretended to eat and not ingested anything today. Otherwise, the guards' feet would be coated in a buffet they'd never seen or inhaled: suckling pig, boiled vicot eggs, tamarind-soaked parpond clams, squash runny with barley, summer rolls, fried banana, grapes, custard topped with raw sugar and pome-granate arils and lavender cake cups—all the items I had hidden in the pot, wide and lidded, buried outside the walls of the food-tasting room. The rest of the meal was in my shirt, as the man next to me suspected.

The other prisoner raised his hands in surrender.

"Sorry," I said to the sentry in submission. "Ache in my stomach."

The mad dash of my heart tempered once the vexed guards withdrew to their positions, but I could no longer direct my attention to the faces of the upper-class ladies or the mature fruits of the tapestry. The neighboring one depicted a fox chasing a rabbit among red flowers. I had one sentiment about it: disturbing. It was easy to read into it and imagine how the red was the blood waiting to flow once the governor, the fox, gave the command to snuff the life of a rabbit like me.

"Please," the man sharing my bench said, in the same low tone as before. In his sad, pleading expression, I saw the certainty of his accursed future more than I felt one for myself.

"Whether imprisoned or beheaded, I prefer a full stomach."

Now, why hadn't I thought the way he did? But his forehead, imprinted with too many lines of hunger worries, reminded me of Sonarus and Ephy. And I had eaten yesterday—three meals and many bites and drinks in between. Each item wasn't served in large portions, but a ladle here and a cup there throughout the day added to the lavishness. Every time any royal member desired a nibble, I was served.

I loosened my drawstrings such that the bread and cheese and a slice of mutton fell into his hands silently, which he then tucked into his clothing.

Where was he going to eat all this food? And when?

"Lestrum! Enter!" A loud voice burst through the left door, and its guard towered over me in ten steps before I gathered myself and stood.

"**D**o you know the reason you are here?" the governor said from behind a long table bearing several items in tidy order.

The room was as grand as his presence. But while one was in a governor's chamber, one didn't idle away time gawking at the surrounding objects when he had pinned you under the stare of his obsidian eyes. So I stood at silent attention.

The Manor had informers around every corner, and I should have kept my arms by my side and my mind from wandering into the wickedness of temptations to avoid this predicament. But dining on rich food available in overabundance several times a day, food that even the cooks or servers were not privileged to indulge in, bred shame and guilt.

At first, my source of distress was the deprived Ashmere folks, but then I worried about the people affected by the Drill's overreach in other parts of our Terra One. And what of other terras? What means had he used to grab rare spices like cloves and saffron, fruits like cabbers or guavas, or seafood found only in the shallow waters elsewhere?

For winds' sake, his citizens couldn't even grow vegetables or fruits in their patch of dirt unless they were granted permission. Drilll owned everything: the food, water, employment, every corner of the house, and every inch of the land underneath it; even the fence surrounding the yard couldn't escape his ownership. And it was the same story with the seeds.

Riddled with compunction, I had conceived an idea. Initially, the notion of smuggling food into the pot had been so frightening I hadn't slept for days before proceeding with the plan. Any noise outside my home, every footfall behind me, and every time my name was uttered in the Manor, I feared exposure. Imaginary shackles, dungeons, and wild dogs intruded on my thoughts the whole time.

On the fated day, I had risen before the sun and reached the Manor in the dark. The earthenware pot I had coveted for days, and which sat by the cookery entryway, was easy to purloin, and the soil, softened by the previous afternoon's rain, was effortless to dig. And before anyone noticed my presence, the pot was in place, concealed, ready to receive.

"Answer!" a female voice with the power to gelatinize a person's insides said. "Didn't you hear my question?"

Timothea! I dared not turn. Besides, why was she in the governor's chamber?

Whatever secret hopes I had of dodging a brutal sentence had rotted; the milk had curdled; the goose had overcooked before the fire turned hot.

"He deserves the harshest punishment," Timothea said to the governor in her high-pitched tone.

Others and I often saw her from the grounds, strolling through the Manor's exterior arcade with her chin held high, pausing under one of the arches, when fancy took her, to scowl at the commoners.

"Lestrum, explain before I pass the sentence," the governor said.

How had they figured out the theft? Had the pot been discovered? Or had someone seen me smuggle the food in it?

"You are giving him a chance to speak?" Timothea's fury rose along with her shrillness, gnashing my nerves. "For what purpose? Father would never do that. Never."

She was irritating.

"Last chance," the governor said. "Speak."

What was there to explain? I had stolen to feed my family. It wasn't right to gorge meal after meal when my wife and child had weekly rations on food and water, which ran out before the next was due. Drilll decided the portions, and men like the one before me executed them.

Ephy and Sonarus never complained, except they never changed their clothes in my presence, lest I see the lack of meat on their bones. I never removed mine in front of them either.

"A life for a life." Timothea's voice cracked like an egg.

My attention peeled off from the governor's table and settled on her shaking head, hidden behind her hands. You shouldn't be so bold, Ephy's modest voice jabbed at me in my mind. You shouldn't be calling her Timothea either, aloud or not.

Timothea's hair, the color of straw used as bedding for barn animals, was as unpliable as her character and presentable only on account of the jewels decorating it. She reacted as if I had stolen those precious stones, her toys.

Once the novelty of Timothea's melting unclenched my concern, and I considered her words, I asked the governor, "A life for a life?"

"Oh! Byron!" Timothea moaned.

A frown slipped onto my face.

"You are the food taster, are you not?" the governor said, not at all blighted by Timothea's runaway emotions.

I nodded.

"Then how is it that the food you sampled did nothing to you but killed Her Ladyship's beau?"

A slice of panic cut through me. This was not a case of theft, but . . . but death!

It wasn't me. Then who was responsible? Someone else had poisoned the food before I had robbed it. My legs felt like dough. The two accusers wanted to know why Byron had died and I'd survived, and not the opposite. What was my purpose if I couldn't prevent such a thing from happening? A life for a life. I understood now.

"I . . . I must have built a tolerance for the poisons. They . . . they did some of that in my training as a food taster." My bound hands clenched against my midriff, and my skin wanted to burst open in a flood of sweat.

"You are deceitful," Timothea shrieked, deafening me for a moment.

Then she strutted to me, her fierce eyes the color of grapes, made brighter by the voluminous hushu gown covering her and matching jewels clutching her neck. They flashed a fresh surge of ire. She was a woman burning with a desire to scorch.

"You poisoned him, didn't you?" she said in a guttural voice, which surprised me.

I shook my head as I realized the additional crime I committed by daring to look at her at close quarters. Foolhardiness was dangerous, but those eyes . . . a pinnacle of beauty . . . so rare. If Ephy had eyes like hers, I would not need food for the rest of my life.

"Then how was Byron taken from me?" Timothea said. "Are you saying that the doctor is wrong?"

How was it that none of the others who'd dined on the food were mentioned? What had Byron eaten that others hadn't? I recalled each item served to me today, trying to decipher flaws in their aroma, their texture. The food stashed in my shirt, and the rest hidden in the pot had seemed ordinary at the time of handling. Was ingestion the only way the poison worked? I unclenched my hands and considered them.

My mind wandered to the hungry man sitting in the antechamber, and the bread, cheese, and mutton I'd handed over. Had I sealed his fate?

"Speak!" The skin beneath Timothea's eyes was dark and swollen, the paleness of her complexion unmissable. "Speeeak!"

I wanted to seal my ears with my palms. I wanted to slap the hysteria out of her.

"I did not poison him," I said with as much courage as I could muster. "I am privileged to have employment as Your Ladyship's food taster. It would serve me in no way to kill him."

Timothea screamed. She marched to the tall window behind the desk and wrenched the curtains off with more force than I had ever seen anyone use. One scream led to another and then another until the governor called upon Timothea's lady-in-waiting to guide her back to her quarters.

Her hysterics rekindled my unease. The prisoner outside, his forehead broader than his jaw and his curly hair too short and sparse to hide his short ears, was ignorant of how his future had changed. A noxious sickness boiled in my stomach.

"You didn't poison Her Ladyship's beau?" the governor said.

"No."

"Are you a conspirator? Working with others to overthrow our overlord?"

"Not at all."

As he paced alongside his table, I gambled a look around the room and its curious possessions. Not one of those grand things lived in mine. My entire home could fit in the chamber and leave space for a complete banquet.

"I don't see a reason you would want to poison him," he said, "so I will give you a lighter ruling."

But before I could spread my smile and offer my gratitude, his next set of words caused my hope and confidence to disappear in a puff of smoke, like straw being dropped in a roaring fire.

"You are to journey to Adivas," he said. "To get the seeds of the rursus tree."

Adivas? Rursus tree? The words sucked the breath out of me. He'd delivered me a death sentence.

Adivas was supposed to be wrapped in an impenetrable belt of a barrier, vicious enough to kill trespassers. Or so the gossip went. And as far as the rursus tree was concerned, it was a mythical tree under which the bravest dared not stand. The pollen that rained day and night could give a nightmarish attack of itching, unstoppable and maddening, and sleep, if it ever came, was fitful and fearsome.

These were bedtime stories for misbehaving children, tales that had traveled generations from tongue to tongue and become so ingrained in our daily lives they were as ordinary as the unpredictable winds of our terra. This was the lore of someone's imagination, created out of boredom, or perhaps in a fury of talent to scare others.

And the man in power had just ordered me to chase it.

"I will ask the cook to pack some food for your travel and get the word out to the stables. A coach is leaving Ashmere after sunset. Prepare to be on it."

"Can I visit my family before I go?"

Ephy would have objected to my question, but how would she know of my errand if I didn't see her? She would assume my demise, killed by some poison, especially when news of Byron's death swept across Ashmere. Granted, I wouldn't be the first person to disappear into obscurity. But knowing Ephy, she would suspect what she reproved most in me: my courage, which often skirted with lack of forethought.

"You won't be allowed to see your family, and if you come back without the seeds . . ." He signaled the guard inside the room to open the door. "You will remain in the servant quarters until your departure."

T he guards struggled to shut the door after the designated people had huddled in the closed coach. Our fickle-minded wind god raged, stirring up gales in his fury. Some guards lost their balance, doors slammed against the side of the coach, and our vehicle rocked, while inside, the sentenced cried out prayers and begged Vavajod for mercy.

"Not an auspicious start," the man sitting across from me said when the situation was brought under control and the coachman directed the two horses out of Ashmere.

"Where are they taking you?" I whispered to the woman beside me.

A silent shiver descended upon her, and she shut her eyes.

They packed ten of us like pickles in a slender vessel: shoulder rubbing shoulder, bottoms on the floor, each headed to a destination as apprehensive as mine.

I tried to engage others in a conversation, but they pretended to go deaf. Perhaps they didn't want an additional charge of plotting against Drilll, lest the coachman divulge. So, I announced I was traveling to Adivas. My news induced them to raise their heads and cast me a wild glance, their countenance bathed in fright—a fear which usually emerges upon a realization that they were in the presence of a man about to die. Even the guards who had learned about my errand today had granted me that look.

Did I imagine my companions leaning away from me? Like death was a disease that could hop from me to them? Then again, one could be held in contempt for talk alone, labeled as a person unsympathetic to Drilll, his wishes and lands.

"If Adivas is real and you find it, how do you plan to get in?" the man across from me whispered.

How would anyone get in anywhere? "Through the gates," I said.

He chuckled. The rest snickered. One snorted. It made my hair stand on its ends, but I nodded, then smiled and laughed in hushed tones like them.

So, if Adivas was real, and if there was no gate, how was I supposed to get in? I repeated the question to myself many times, in between the amusement I had provided to the coach's gloomy interiors and until the coachman had divested himself of my company.

During the journey, the heat was excessive, making the air inside the windowless space oppressive and hard to breathe despite the howling winds outside, heating the food the guards had given me and spoiling it. Yet the chill at night had no trouble worming its way in through the cracks and crevices. My limbs were stiff from being stationary in the cramped space and my behind was sore.

Then there was the jostling of the coach. Constant bumping and pushing and shoving brought on an unfamiliar weariness, like someone had beaten me with a rolling pin to their heart's content. Out of the many roads running away from the Manor property, like spokes of a wheel, only four were paved, and they stretched in the cardinal directions, mostly ignoring the mainways crisscrossing the continent. Now, why wouldn't the coachman choose a crude one when smooth roads were available? It was the best way to further our misery.

And when the wheel failed on the rugged road, long after the other prisoners had gotten off, I was made to mount saddleless on a horse and follow the coachman, plodding on dirt paths cutting through Ashmere's farmlands girdling the city. There, in the weak light of early morning, folks hunched over, whether for weeding, planting, or harvesting, I couldn't tell, but their postures defined overburden and resignation. The ones handling the ox-pulled plows were as silent as others. They lifted their heads, their hair whipping about, as we passed through, but we exchanged no greetings.

Throughout the confusing time of being led north on horseback, then east, zigzagging back north, later crossing the Whirly River and continuing on, hunger and thirst were my constant companions.

The worst, however, was the absence of words and expressions. Other occupants were more comfortable with close mouths and stoic faces, and I tolerated it initially, except as each prisoner got off at their designated location, the emptiness bit me. And after the last occupant left and before the coach broke, the silence activated my agonies and fermented into lunacy. In those moments, I understood Timothea's hysteria—her need to scream.

But I was a man, Drilll and his family's food taster, still a commoner. Screaming like Timothea would not make the coachman return me to my quarters. I clung to my sanity, same as the way my paunch held my grumbling stomach.

As the coachman sorted his way, keeping the horses steady against God Vavajod's tantrums and avoiding the ruts in the roads and pits dug at their edges, I contemplated the bulge in his saddlebag pockets. Not the clip-clop, nor the neighing of the horses could mask the sloshing of water. It made a particular madness foam up to the surface, made worse by the cruelty of the sun.

"Go!" the coachman said after I dismounted, pointing in the direction of the Meltwater Mountain Range which divided the northern part of Terra One into eastern and western halves. Surely he didn't mean for me to proceed there. The range was too far to even be visible from Ashmere, a city in the central lands, closer to the western boundary of the continent.

"Which way?" I said, only to be frowned upon.

"What do I care."

I couldn't move, my feet an extension of the cakey ground beneath me.

"Should I go beyond that parcel of land?"

"You know what you are supposed to do." He turned his horses around and flicked his hand as if swatting a fly. "Go now."

"Our meals spoiled because of the heat." My eyes settled on the bulge.

He began his journey back.

"Can I have something to drink?" I left my desire for food unspoken.

The coachman's eyes were cold, dressed with disdainful contempt. If the governor had supplied him a weapon, he wouldn't have hesitated to brandish it, like a butcher wouldn't with a doomed guinea fowl. But I had to survive until I found Adivas and its nonexistent gate.

He tossed a water sac and trotted off with the extra horse in tow.

B eyond the pastureland, more farms—not yet captured by our ruler—abutted each other. Not a soul came into sight. The afternoon sun usually drove people indoors. Alas, Ashmere folks weren't so lucky.

Upon finding a well, I quenched my thirst and refilled my water sac before splashing a bucket of cold water over me. Nearby trees had ripe fruit to satiate me. When done, I wedged as many as I could fit in my shirt and resumed the same route until doubt cast its heavy shadow and filled me with worry.

I had changed directions twice and trudged for several hours before the day closed. Come night, the air chilled, and I sought refuge on a farm. The farmer allowed me to rest on a bundle of hay in a barn warmed by the animals, and his wife handed me nourishment. It was luxury compared to the night in the coach.

With a half-day gone in walking the next day, panic wrapped me like the easterly winds. What did the barrenness of the land and sparsity of people and housing mean? What was north of Ashmere? Why had Drilll, eager by nature, ceased his advance in that direction?

Blasting winds! I was headed toward the Restless Barrens—the largest desert to exist among all seven terras—toward the dead expanse of sand where shifting dunes and sandstorms and sand funnels abounded, toward Vavajod's playground.

Throwing an impatient huff, I glanced at the distant remains of Drilll's city for a few breaths. I would have changed course had it not been for the farmer's vague hints. So, I cleared my parched throat and headed toward a cluster of trees, battered and exhausted by the tearing gusts blowing out of the Restless Barrens. Beyond, there were thorny bushes and wild vegetation.

Soon I got to a hedgerow, as green as quick-cooked asparagus. On and on, it continued either side as far as my vision stretched, towering three feet above me. The verdant wall comprised one type of plant whose branches—as broad as my wrists—tangled together to make an impenetrable thicket. Hooked thorns sprung from the stalks, along with fat, fleshy pads resembling a vicious claw. What kind of hedgerow was this?

I plodded on, my boots kicking dust, the sun proceeding across the sky.

How would those meaty pads taste with some lard and onions?

Nothing provided an escape from the heat. Sweat beads rolled from my forehead and stung my eyes, and my shoes were like tiny ovens roasting my feet. I licked my drying lips and tasted salt. An outburst of desire to pluck one of those pads and chew it raw drove my hand to the thicket. Except . . . what if the plants were poisonous?

I drew back.

Wouldn't that be funny? Looking at my rotund body, lifeless from a seized heart, the onlookers would remark on how my mad cravings had driven me to devour thorns and noxious plants to satiate the meat and fat on my bones.

"Didn't the Manor feed him enough?" they would say, shaking their heads. "Once a food taster, always a food taster. In the Manor or the wild."

I would become a cautionary tale, a nighttime story to subdue naughty children akin to the rursus trees and their pollen. I would have laughed at the notion had Ephy's image not flashed before me: hard at work at the brick ovens, absorbing the heat, fumes, and the soot from the wood fires, her body driven by a meager meal of carrots with rye porridge in a meat broth consumed the night prior.

I gnashed my teeth. Why couldn't Drilll order the use of sorghum blocks for intense and efficient fires like other terras? He had the means to get them. Perhaps he could use cheaper, lower-quality par-par blocks instead if his silver spards and gold crowns were too precious to him. But wood was his choice because making his people toil and suffer was his intention.

My errand became tolerable after that, and I ceased my complaining.

By the time the sun was a few hours away from setting, I had found a break in the hedge in the form of a brick wall—low and maintained. A canal furrowed from the wall, away from me, through the green barrier.

I gasped in delight. The canal brimmed with the very substance the sun had toiled to extract and rob from me. Depositing myself on the wall, I lowered my face to feel the coolness rise off the surface. The still water smelled fruity, reminding me of pomegranates. I studied my reflection for a moment. Apart from the weariness and striking shabbiness, the hardship had not touched my form. My face was as round and full as before. Then, as I was about to dunk my hand in the deliciousness to scoop some thirst-quenching liquid, I noted a sudden and restless movement underneath.

"Fish!" I said aloud. "The day's getting better and better."

But when my fingers grazed the surface, I noticed their teeth: long enough to match half the length of my fingers and powerful enough to break bones. The fish pressed together in the water closer to me. Their restlessness made sense now; they were aware of my presence.

My trust in the wall crumbled, and I jumped off, remembering the creaking bench. I shuddered despite the heat.

Adivas had to be real. And this was *it*.

The sun got closer to the horizon as I tried to develop solutions for my quandary. Passing the night under the stars was a horrible idea for two definite reasons: my clothing was inadequate protection against the cold, and there was a substantial likelihood of my body becoming a juicy meal should some outlandish creature emerge from the hedge. Perhaps the latter was imaginary, but then so was Adivas. Besides, weren't the bizarre hedge plants and the peculiar fish proof enough?

As I mulled over the prospects of my mission's success, I found a man in a long, slender boat approaching. The day was turning riper by the hour. The rower was in no apparent hurry, a sharp contrast to what lurked underneath his boat.

An unusual feeling of caution stirred. I had no weapons, but if trouble ensued, I could use my weight as one since the man was half my width.

"Declare your intent," the man called out to me from afar.

Would they let me in if I told the truth? Ephy's voice urged prudence.

"I come in peace," I said.

"Do you have weapons?"

I stretched my arms toward the sky. The man advanced.

"Is this Adivas?" I said.

"Why does it matter? We don't allow strangers to enter our village, so go away."

"Overlord Drilll send me."

"Your overlord doesn't rule here." He slowed his paddling. "Leave. Unless you want to be shot."

He stabilized his single-bladed paddle on his thighs and nocked an arrow in his bow while his vessel glided ahead with ease, weightless and noiseless.

It wasn't easy to ignore his warning nor to suppose what laced the pointy end of the arrowhead. However, I had nowhere to go. On the occasion that I returned to Ashmere without fulfilling the governor's demand, I was an imprisoned man, if not dead. A fatal arrow in the free land while breathing clean air was better than being hanged or caged in dungeons reeking of the rancid smell of piss and feces and death.

I squeezed my eyes. Which way would I fall?

"It's you!" he said. "I can't believe it! It is you—Lestrum!"

When I opened my eyes, he was close enough to be recognized: a man with a large head on a slender frame, forehead broader than the chin, and short ears, the same from the antechamber.

"I wanted to thank you, but I never thought I would see you again." The moment the front of the boat touched the wall, he was over the hurdle, binding me with his arms. "Your generosity renewed my desire to live. I'm alive because of you!"

Alive? His presence fuddled my brain. I slumped to the dirt, not pretty for someone my size, but I was on the ground. The heat, the thirst, the hunger, were unhinging me. Earlier, when I'd thought my senses had taken leave of me, I must have been just woolgathering, not going insane. What I was feeling now was true insanity. How long could a man last without sustenance? A man whose gut received three or more satisfying meals per day?

My cheeks stung, and my shirt and mouth were wet with water when I regained my senses. The man didn't need to convince me to ride with him to his village, although the narrowness of a piece of wood serving as a seat gave me a bundle of jitters—my body in his slender boat . . . the devilish fish below.

"Is this Adivas?" I stiffened like a piece of day-old bread once I settled behind him, afraid to make any movement.

Were they short on wood? Was that why his boat was so narrow?

"This is Adivas, and my name is Bhuja." The rowing was seamless, as though the paddle was an extension of his arms; each stroke created a tiny splash and a dimple in the water, which he then pushed behind with ease.

This man from Adivas was beside me on the bench across the tapestries, right outside the chamber of the man who'd sent me on this chase.

The whole trouble could have been taken care of within minutes. If only we had been together in the governor's room when he had punished me . . .

The air was humid, and insects trilled despite the Barrens being a few miles from here.

"Why are you not locked in a dungeon?" I said. "And why were you in Ashmere in the first place?"

The spiny hedge was remarkable. It grew from the water and ran deeper inland, more of a field than a fence. Any thought of bundling up in hardy clothes and dashing through it to reach Adivas was a call to death. My clothes would be shredded within a few steps into the thicket; next would be the skin and muscles; the emotional sinew would be long gone before that.

"The overlord's guards found me outside my village."

"This far from Ashmere? Aren't these free lands?"

"They said they were going toward Windrose," Bhuja said. "They became suspicious of my attire, captured me, took me to Ashmere, and threw me in the dungeon to await sentencing. Five days and nights without food and with scarce water made me resign myself to the inevitable. But then I found you. You reversed my thinking. An opportunity for escape presented itself, and I took it."

"An opportunity to escape?" I said. "Do you know how rare that is?"

"With all the guards everywhere and everyone watching each other, I believe you. It serves me right for leaving my village."

Being taller than the rower afforded me the same view as him, and I discerned land and trees ahead.

"After I slipped away, I found a coach leaving Ashmere that evening, and I hung onto the undercarriage unseen."

"You were underneath us the entire time?" My shock rocked the boat. I gripped the sides, breath stuck halfway in my throat, eyes piercing the water, staring at the monsters lying in wait below.

"No, just for a day. Then I found a merchant who allowed me space in his wagon."

Six days of inadequate food and water had driven me to lunacy, so hanging on to the undercarriage after days of similar deprivation was beyond my comprehension. I couldn't even tolerate resting my bottom on the horse for a few hours, and here he was rowing a stout companion as if he had never set foot in Ashmere. Also, how had he gotten to Adivas before me?

"Did you use magic for that?"

He burst out laughing. "You must have taken the long way to get here."

Before I could question him on how Adivas differed from Changewinds, our boat came to a stop at grass-covered land. My behavior was like when Ephy and Sonarus had seen the spread of food before them, the fare that I had pilfered and brought home for the first time. Their eyes were as big as the plates housed in the Manor. They'd never seen food like that before, never experienced such a bounty, so they didn't know where to look.

Dwellings and essential buildings, stumpy and of varied sizes, were scattered on land larger than Manor grounds. Like most homes in Terra One, the structures were six-sided huts, with their west-facing walls being the strongest and devoid of any breaks where westerly wind could enter and cause problems. Their roofs had multiple slopes and minimal overhangs, and only the east wall bore the entrances. It was obvious these were built on the strength of willing men and good fellowship, and this was a place where fear couldn't threaten peace of mind. My shoulders relaxed.

The houses of Ashmere, in contrast, faced every which way, their roofs designed for places other than Terra One. Drilll was from a different terra and cared little about our mercurial god Vavajod blowing in from the Gamnia Oceans of the west. So, homes were in neat rows radiating away from the Manor, broken by concentric streets—akin to a spider's web—giving it an ordered but senseless feel.

As I exited the boat, I thought I was living a dream where no guards existed. Old-fashioned clothing and shoes, similar to Bhuja's, were everywhere. Some people went about their chores, and others socialized while children sang, hopped, and skipped. Their skin spoke of a sun-blessed existence, and their faces told a story of contentment and ease of living.

Life had been as simple as this in Changewinds. Sure, my parents, siblings, and I had to work hard to survive, but we'd never starved. We took pride in our vocation, and when we retired for the night, dreams, not nightmares, filled our sleep. To think that my situation had improved from the pig-rearing times was a folly. My chest felt heavy and a yearning for the past kindled. Alas, it was unreachable now.

A nectarous fragrance of custard tickled my nostrils. It had an undertone of delicate elderflowers and honey-sweetened almond milk. Fresh and gentle, it impregnated the air. I searched for the source.

A special strip of land girdled Adivas on the inside of the thorny hedge, broken only by the patches of ground abutting the canals. On this strip flourished mature trees, standing erect in pride and confidence like the governor's guards, their branches tortuous against the drowning light of the sky. And their yellow-green leaves were like the children of Adivas: cheery, carefree, and dancing nonstop to the tunes of Vavajod.

"These are our precious rursus trees," Bhuja said from behind me.

"Did you say rursus?"

"The ones before us."

"Rursus?"

"Yes."

"They exist," I murmured.

"Only in Adivas," he said.

They existed. They were real!

As I raced to those living sculptures, the men tried to stop me, but the trees' beauty and fragrance enticed me.

"You are not a fantasy," I said under my breath.

Someone pulled my arms and told me to halt, but I resisted and hugged the trunk, the color of bricks and with the velvety softness of the Manor chairs.

Yellow dust rained over me. The airy flakes swirled in tight circles in response to the breeze, and it made me giddy with delight. I glimpsed the snatches of blue through the patchwork of leaves and thought their branches were holding the sky.

The men screamed at me.

Why would I stop when luck had discovered me? Here I was, under the same tree I'd had no hopes of finding. And what generosity. Trees lined up as far as my eye could reach. No death awaited me, and I could return to Ashmere and see my family. I grinned; I twirled; I rejoiced.

Seeds . . . I had to get them. I stilled and searched among the foliage hanging above me.

Meanwhile, a fire billowed through my skin like I was some game, skinned, skewered, and roasted on a spit. Its intensity piled and piled. I fell back against the trunk and slid down. Bhuja was upon me, yelling something I couldn't decipher. Other men rushed around me.

My hands were the color of lemons, and so were my clothes.

The men carried me. I was too distressed to count the number of people my bulk required. The burn dug into my bones and sinews, slow and agonizing. Did Ephy ever get licked by the flames where she toiled? If she had, she had never shown me the scars.

By the time they brought me inside a hut, the misery had finished one pass and returned for seconds. I howled as the pain bloomed, then I vomited as my body shook, and soon after, I returned to shrieking. The agony crawled from one phase to another and back again, over and over.

I could have cast my guts out from constant heaving had not someone smacked me on the head.

When I regained consciousness, burning was replaced by what the rursus trees were reputed for, and no matter how hard I scratched, I could never quite reach the itch to quench it. It was everywhere—even in unreachable places, like my bones and behind my eyes and deep inside my chest. The itch worsened each time I dragged in a breath.

Their reaction was to tie my arms and legs to the cot. How cruel. Why didn't they leave me alone and let me scratch?

Then, when the villagers untied me, they forced the vilest-tasting liquid remedies on me each time I awoke. How could they expect my stomach, coddled with Manor delicacies, to handle such horrid-tasting liquid? Where were the sweet custard and almond milk that I had gotten a whiff of earlier?

One time I awoke drenched in sweat; another time, crying. Twice I roused in the middle of an episode of thrashing, breaking a child's arm during one of them. The scariest, however, was when I regained consciousness amid a nightmare: the food at the Manor table had come alive, untamed and ferocious, and instead of me gorging on them, they assaulted me and attempted to devour me whole. "Diabolical!" I cried out over and over until the villagers forced their drinks on me again.

I didn't know the total amount of brew I consumed, nor how many days had passed by the time the itch became bearable and the villagers permitted me to become conscious. The yellow was gone, and my skin was back to its original shade, dressed in old-fashioned clothing. People and objects lost their haziness.

Then they fed me. Not with the rare delicacies of the Manor kitchen, but with nourishing meals, solid enough to strengthen a man whose weight had melted like candle wax.

"I have to go back," I said as soon as I could speak.

A low murmur of surprise spread around me because the villagers knew that my recovery was not complete. The elders and Bhuja had crammed into the hut in which I was recovering, its windows and door framing the additional faces of those who couldn't fit inside.

"Why did you come here to begin with?" Bhuja said.

I hesitated to tell them my story and was even tempted to twist it, but slyness didn't come easy to me.

"My punishment was to get here and bring the seeds of the rursus tree to the governor."

The men cried in unison, then fell silent. Outrage sprouted on their faces and rose off like vapors, thickening the surrounding air. If their stares were knives, I would have been a heap of pieces on the earthen floor.

Bhuja showed his dislike and anger in a quiet, controlled way. "We allowed you into Adivas because you were kind to me. It is one of the foundational values we hold in high esteem, besides trust, respect, and responsibility. What you ask for now shows your greed, which we cannot oblige. By acknowledging our village's existence, by allowing you to enter, and by saving your life, we have returned the favor. We have nothing more to give."

"We will pack you some food for your journey back," an elder said, his jaw tight like the rest.

"No, I can't go back without the seeds. I will be skinned." I wiped my hands on my shirt to rid them of sweat. "You have met the governor. His cordial disposition is a shell."

"Our concern is to protect this village and preserve our way of life," Bhuja said. "Scarlet cannot have more than what he has already grabbed."

"Who's Scarlet?"

"You probably haven't been outside Ashmere for a while, have you?" He paused for me to agree. "Steeped in the blood of so many Terra Oners, your overlord has earned a nickname."

"It wouldn't surprise me if he scored many labels."

"Seeds can't leave Adivas, though," Bhuja said. "We *cannot* back torture and bloodshed."

"But my family is unaware of my journey here." I choked at the thought of Ephy and Sonarus's loss and the resulting sadness. "I will never get to see them again."

The villagers abandoned me. What remained in the hut were my clothes, an evening meal, the cot, and me on it.

The door framed a rursus tree and a ring of yellow beneath it. Its fragrance wafted in, mixing with those of the herbs hanging from the rafters in various stages of drying. How could a tree so dreaded in the lands far and wide be regarded with such respect and honor that the mere suggestion of sharing its seeds was offensive? All the trees did was bring trouble. Or was I mistaken?

Light and shadows played with the branches and the leaves, and puffs of wind made the pollen fly. The tree's vigor and strength were undeniable. As the sun retired, its soft and diffused light awarded a warm glow to the stalwart's graceful lines, its velvety bark darkening and taking on a sheen, reminding me of silky, lush wine. It was a wonder, unexpected and overpowering, a beauty which dwarfed that of Timothea's eyes. Ephy, who adored sceneries and seascapes, would have rejoiced at the sight.

Then, long after the crickets began their choruses, the moon climbed and silvered the tree, outlining its striking features against the night sky. The pollen still swirled in soft waves, hazing the sharp outlines, and the leaves continued their whispers, soothing my misery. The rursus appeared so majestic, so hardy. It bewitched me, swelling my heart with bliss and awe. I realized why reverence was a fitting sentiment.

But the truth remained: I had failed my task.

The villagers' answer was as clear as the water in their canals. I had assumed too much and asked for more than I had shared. My mind, exhausted and incapable of reasoning, failed at producing any cunning plans. I was never prudent or long-sighted anyway. I'd told the villagers forthrightly what I desired, and by doing so, I'd insulted them. Tears formed and trickled, wetting my loaned shirt.

At daybreak, I awoke to a packed hut once again. No fantastical beings were set loose in my dreams, but neither had my slumber been profound or restful. I was tired and still mending from my ailment.

Their faces were solemn. A fresh bowl of porridge and greens sat next to the previous night's untouched meal by the cot's leg. *Eat, change back into your clothes, and go* was what I read in their expressions.

Or were they here to submit a charge and demand reparation?

"Why were you exiled?" Bhuja sat by my feet. He wasn't the head of the village, but the men whose bodies were marked in wrinkles and foreheads in wisdom had chosen him as their spokesperson.

Because Timothea's beau died from poisoning, I could have said, but I was not responsible for that villainy. "I stole food for my family. Some of which I gave to you."

A murmur spread through the crowd.

"How loyal are you to Scarlet?" Bhuja said. "Remember, we hold the truth in high regard here."

"Nobody is more important to me than my family."

The elders nodded.

"You seem to hold an important position in Scarlet's household," Bhuja said.

They were unaware of my role in Ashmere Manor. Had I never mentioned it to Bhuja?

"I am . . . I was their food taster." A person whose life is useful to Drilll's household until poison appears in the sole luxury he is afforded, his fate decided by an assassin. A life he didn't own. Someone who was replaceable. "I'm not important."

"Are your wife and son as honest and considerate as you are?"

"I would be a lesser man if not for them."

The elders gestured with their heads at each other and to Bhuja.

"Can I tell you why we honor rursus trees here?" Bhuja said.

"Please."

"In the early days, Scarlet's father, Druchaddd, was in power. When his soldiers marched through and seized territory after territory, they tried occupying an entire region dotted with rursus trees. But trouble awaited them. They blamed the witches' hexes and sand-demons when their men fell victim to the pollen's influence.

"Generations living in and around the region knew about the unusual trees and had avoided farming or grazing their animals in the area. Still, when unable to steer clear of Druchaddd's men and pressed for answers, the natives denied knowledge about the source of the soldiers' sickness. Yet Druchaddd persisted. He kept sending his men. Each new batch came flaunting its overbearing pride and ability. Most died with no one tending them in their torment, but a few recovered and some who had the sense to protect themselves fled in fear. Eventually, the tyrant gave up. And the natives and the land remained uncaptured.

"Our fathers and grandfathers were those natives. They were stubborn and refused to bow to the will of Druchaddd. Once the soldiers abandoned their hopes of capture, the people formed a community on the values we continue to respect today.

"Healers among them knew how to stave off the pollen's worst effects, to build resistance against it. They were familiar with the trees' life cycle, knew that the fruits were borne every eight to ten years. So, what seeds they had saved from previous years, they planted.

"The trees surrounding our land are those trees, and the ground on which our village exists is the same region the soldiers abandoned. So, you see, because the trees saved our ancestors' lives and each generation's after theirs, we are forever in their debt."

Their story captured me.

"They protect us from the ruler of Ashmere and his men," Bhuja continued. "They also provide us shade and are living spaces for birds, insects, and small animals. Their fruit—"

"Fruit?" The old me would have salivated at the thought.

"It's the size of a large apple," Bhuja continued. "The outer skin is yellow and tough. The pulpy middle layer is bitter and used fresh and dried as medicine for different ailments. And the inner shell, which the birds and small animals love to crack open to get to the seed, we use in our fires for cooking. Since the trees fruit at long intervals, the fruits are plentiful and packed with seeds. If we can get them before the creatures do, they are delicious when roasted. We grind the seeds and use the powder as a thickener in our meals."

"I thought the trees and what they did were folktales," I said, spellbound.

"It doesn't surprise us. Our people never disclosed the secrets, for obvious reasons. And except for the runaway soldiers of the past, no one has seen the trees and verified their existence. So whatever stories made it out there got passed about as folklore."

"Do rursus trees exist anywhere outside Adivas?"

"We sent our men far and wide to search for them, but they only uncovered rumors and tall tales. If saplings are found from the seeds carried by birds or animals, we destroy them. We don't want them to fall into Scarlet's hands."

"What about the plants with the padded, clawed leaves?" I said.

"Sher panja? Our ancestors found those growing beside a neglected pond and put them to good use as a hedgerow. Their growth is frenzied, which we use to our advantage."

"How do you restrain it?"

"What else? We eat it. We brine and pickle the pads and the stems. They taste good with onions and fowl."

Hadn't the idea occurred to me? I could be one of Adivas's cooks.

"Their lavender flowers are used when tartness is needed. Its plump red fruit, the length of your thumb, is crunchy and cooling against the heat when eaten raw. It tastes like honeyed cherries when ripe, which is worthwhile because cherries can't grow here."

Nothing got wasted here. My admiration for the villagers and their way of living was renewed.

"We don't do this often," Bhuja said, and people around us nodded. "But when we find people who reflect our values, we offer them a proposition. Are you willing to leave Ashmere and settle in Adivas for good? With your family?"

My thoughts about food and the villagers' cleverness and resourcefulness went blank. What had he said? Despite the engaging conversation, I had been awaiting a fine, an act of revenge bathed in contempt, their demand for penance. Not this . . . I couldn't understand . . . it was as if the villagers had poured the food of the Goddesses and that of wind god Vavajod into my chipped clay chalice, filling it to the brim and letting it overflow.

Nobody had bestowed such charity on me. Ephy and Sonarus would forever be free from the torment of Drilll's rules and restrictions. It brought back memories of Changewinds when benevolence was not in such scarcity. And with the memories came tears.

I sobbed into my hands. And when they were soaked, I wept on Bhuja's shoulders.

The villagers had directed me to the principal route to Ashmere. It was bustling with coaches and wagons and horses, and it didn't take me long to get passage to the city.

Closed and loaded with cloth goods, the inside of the coach was dingy and its air oppressive. Who wouldn't find the confinement grievous after breathing the fragrance of Adivas? Yet lightness surrounded me. An ever-present burden had lifted from my mind, and an ingrained apprehension had loosened its claws. Of course, some of it was from the weight I had shed. More importantly, Drilll's grasp on my spirit had disengaged.

I unclenched my grip on the wooden box secured in my trouser pocket.

My life would soon be my own. I would live for Ephy and Sonarus and no one else.

"**G**overnor is occupied. Give the seeds to me." Manacles jangled in the guard commander's hands, ready for use.

"I want to go home to my family." Hope allowed me to breach my boundaries, to the point of being whipped.

"Are you trying to bargain with me?" He shackled my hands.

"Make sure you have another set of shackles for you as well." Fury made me bolder and more imprudent—a pitfall I was born with, but because of the morsels in my hand, I had the power to sway people and outcomes. "Never mind the shackles. If the governor knows you have wasted an opportunity for His Lordship to possess a rare weapon, you might be cleaved right then."

"Give me the seeds, then!"

"They are not any old seeds." I shoved my bound hands toward his midsection, my eyes on the ring of keys in his hand. "And the governor won't be pleased if you touch them or the box."

He freed me with reluctance and brought me to the governor's antechamber. Although I had returned to where it had begun, it wasn't the same. The bench no longer creaked in complaint at my weight. The fruit on the tapestry, so appetizing earlier, seemed overripe and distasteful. And in the fox-chasing-the-rabbit-among-the-red-flowers tapestry, I detected ample space and routes for the rabbit's escape. Then, when the guard sporting the shiny breastplate and helmet brought me into the governor's chamber, I realized how limited his space was compared to the land hemmed in by the rursus trees and how scanty his heart was when judged against those of the villagers.

"I brought you the seeds."

"You didn't need to see me for that." The governor sat behind his table, distracted by papers.

"I want to leave Ashmere with my family."

He pinned me with his glare, papers forgotten, showing no sign of surprise at the change in my appearance.

"I can give you the seeds, but they won't grow."

"Why not?" He walked to me.

"Because you won't be able to handle them to grow them. And nor will His Lordship. The seeds have the same quality as the trees are famed for." The memory of the agony I had endured on Adivas—the dues I had paid for my freedom—came rushing back.

"Where do you plan to go? Adivas?" He laughed.

I didn't share his amusement.

"My family and a coach to help us are all I want in return." I was at my never-surpassed height of brazenness, the likes of which the governor had not encountered in his lifetime. All he had to do was flick his finger at the guard, and moments later, I would be on the floor senseless and the halberd steeped in red. But the governor was too distracted to rebuke me.

"Show them to me." In his extended arm, I saw Ephy's stretched arm, securing the meager rations brought to our street every Sunday.

Soon my wife would no longer need the governor's charity.

I untucked the square box from my shirt, seeds rattling within as the box changed hands. A cloud of sweet custard, elderflowers, and honey-sweetened almond milk dispersed through the room when the governor opened the lid. Its intensity was so unexpected, his grip on the box grew clumsy. And had I not held out my hands underneath his, he would have dropped the box.

He hadn't thought I could do it. It was written all over his face. I realized he knew Adivas existed, that it wasn't lore, and he had sent me out there thinking otherwise. Such satisfaction was to be had in disconcerting someone sheathed in layers of untouchable power.

For the next few moments, the yellow seeds—the size of my nails—became his world. They had him breathless, just like the yellow rain from the trees had me entranced.

He would not refuse my request. I had brought something of immense significance to him and Drilll, historic even. In his expression, I read the hunger for victories in wars they never fathomed winning, the greed of procuring unknown lands, new riches, and power, and the fruition of all other unachievable wishes they had never dreamed. It was possible with the help of an unparalleled weapon he held in his grip. He couldn't but surrender to my demand.

"How do I know this is not pretension?"

"Rub them, and you will see."

His fingers twitched, but he refrained. "I'll grant your request once you tell me how to handle and grow them." He closed the box.

"What guarantee do I have that the guards will not capture me and send me to the dungeons the moment I part with that knowledge?"

I'm sure he had experienced the commoners' distrust before, but the one that hung between us was barefaced and unavoidable. He could imprison me or slaughter me, but then he wouldn't have the answers. Could he take the risk?

"I'll divulge the secret at Ashmere's boundary," I said. "Provided no guards accompany our coach, and nobody follows us once we exit."

As he deliberated over his dilemma, I inhaled the delightful scent in the air. I was glad I wasn't the one deciding because pleasing Drilll was difficult, whether one was common folk or higher in the ranks of His Lordship's army. However, this governor had lasted for several years longer than the previous, showing how his values aligned with the despot and the despot's with his.

"I'll have you and your family executed if you are dishonest." His obsidian eyes were attempting to seek, reach in, and grab my soul.

"Agreed."

As I exited the Manor, I learned about my replacement. What would his fate be? The guards had yet to capture the offender who had poisoned Timothea's beau. And if another death occurred, what penalty would the governor impose on this substitue?

I wished to help this new man, but the guards followed me until I was off the Manor grounds. Besides, I was devoid of means and power and subjected to the same harshness as others, so how could I assist, even if my heart was brimming with desire?

Putting aside the worry about the one succeeding me, I went home on buoyant feet.

I could have asked for additional favors, but my greed could have snatched away the governor's boon and left me empty-handed, so I forced myself to be content with a coach driving us to the outskirts of Ashmere.

My family knew nothing about my ordeal, and I would keep it a mystery until we reached safety. A leak about my unusual journey to Adivas could threaten our freedom. The guard commander, perched next to the coachman—both separated from us by a dense woven cloth—had ears as keen as a wolf's.

I trusted no one, not even the coachman who was a neighbor. The governor knew how to use people; his resentfulness, lack of conscience, and his skill with deceitful tricks made him good at it. My neighbor drove to our house and stood outside our door, unnecessarily guarding it, during which time his ears belonged solely to the governor.

Ephy inquired several times in whispers, but I pointed to the coach's front and shook my head. Sonarus wrinkled his brow and kept pinching the skin of his throat as he stared at me. When I wrapped my arm around his slight frame and smiled, he dared to ask questions, although the tightness in his shoulders and the tremor in his voice lingered.

For him, I had changed, not just in body but in expression, and my usual cheer had turned into a somber mood. We were being whisked away somewhere for a reason I was afraid to disclose. He wept. Ephy diverted his attention with stories and songs until we ate, and then a quick game of noughts and crosses uplifted him.

We chose the direct course, but it was still too long and demanding for Sonarus. Ephy and I didn't fare well either. Our legs and joints were stiff and our muscles cramped when we exited at our destination. A smaller wagon waited in the shadow of a boulder by a crossroad. My family regarded it with suspicion, but I pressed my palm against my heart and breathed a quick prayer to the Goddesses upon seeing it. An urgent want of freedom rushed in.

"So, out with the secret." The guard commander jumped off his seat and eyed the approaching smaller wagon with disbelief.

The guards of Ashmere were impatient, and their commander twice as much, but now that we had the upper hand, I made him wait until Ephy and Sonarus settled in the wagon.

"Tell His Lordship to slather his hands in oil before he touches them. To let the seeds warm in his hands before sowing them one finger's length deep in the soil. And not to trust them to anyone else, because I won't be getting more for him if they go missing."

"That's it?" The guard commander frowned.

"Should I embellish the truth with falsities just to please you?" I stepped into the covered wagon.

"His Lordship will order your capture and torture if you lie!" he yelled to our wagon's posterior.

I poked my head through the window as our driver sped his horses. "You have my whole-hearted permission."

The guard commander pursued us. Did anyone doubt who had given the order? But we were far ahead when they started, and our wagon was smaller and lighter, our horses healthier and brisker. We lost them to dust in a short while.

I n the time it took us to reach Adivas, my joy returned, and I shared about the trials I'd undergone. My wife and child listened with gaping mouths, many emotions crossing their faces.

"That was the best story you've ever told me," Sonarus said.

"He's been practicing storytelling," Ephy said to our son, sneaking a glance at me.

"Will the villagers of Adivas have other wonderful tales for me when we get there?" Sonarus asked.

"Plenty more." I thought of the merry children. "But who needs stories when great friends are to be had?"

"What was in the villagers' drink that helped you?" Ephy said.

"Many things, but mainly the bark of the very tree that caused the ailment."

"The Adivasians must have loved you," my son said. "So much that they shared their dear seeds with the overlord."

I leaned back against the side of the wagon, my cheeks warming with pleasure.

"They were not real seeds." I chuckled at the inventiveness of the villagers.

"What then?" Ephy asked in puzzlement.

"Just the rursus pollen packed in the shape of seeds."

Their breaths hitched.

"Oil or no oil," I said. "the pollen will do its work, and Drilll will suffer. And in his situation, there'll be no remedy."

Ephy didn't grimace or glower or correct me for calling the overlord by his name in our son's presence. Instead, she laughed and laughed, and her face shone like the moon I had witnessed from the hut.

"Your boldness is not so foolish after all," she said and pinched my cheeks.

2

THE SPLINTERED SECRET

Mother issued warnings regularly, so as she finished binding my hair with black ribbons, wrapped a scarf around the arrangement, and said, "Sukhi, don't expose your head to anyone," I nodded by rote habit. My mind was in the clutches of the breeze wafting through the window. Sugar-laden, the air tickled my nostrils and lured my taste buds.

She dragged my chin toward her. "Are you listening? No one should see your hair."

To appease her, I tossed her an acknowledgment a second time, then slipped my shoes on, collected my school supplies, and heeding the call of tart fruitiness, I hurried out of the house and headed for Burned Mill Road before Mother could fuss about packing lunch. Pained at the thought of my lateness, I rushed, short-winded.

The shops, single-leveled and squat, hunkered shoulder to shoulder on either side of the trade road stretching from the southern end of Bisamburi, my neighborhood, to the city's northern shore. For some obscure reason, our school Mercy Terrace sat defiant and unapologetic amid the rolling hills and paved roads and grand houses of the north. Constant discontent about it streamed out of the northerners and was an argument-arousing subject for our parents. But for me, it was about the sights and sounds on the way there.

Shop owners had already unlocked and thrown their doors open for buyers. As always, the area was awash in the full spectrum of the rainbow, each building competing for consideration just as much as the businesses housed in them. What a delightful sight to enjoy, not once but twice, back and forth from my school. These buildings were similar to confetti at parties, the ones we had at Mercy Terrace, three times a year. The hues were so vivid, so refreshing, brighter still when the early rays of the sun hit them. They never faded. The merchants didn't allow them.

The colors, also, reminded me of the old painting hung front and center in our school's lofty foyer: a motley of pigments in streaks and blotches, haphazard in its form, wild in its flow, its garishness tamed only by the shafts of light from windows perched above the main door, high and mighty.

It was early still. The market road, usually bustling with energy by noon, was empty of throngs of shoppers and passersby and devoid of the congestion caused by the northern cabs. As I advanced, I kept my object-of-interest in my vision: the structure whose chimney billowed puffs of candied flavors and whose outside glistened in robin's-egg blue. It was my favorite shop.

Mother sent me to school for the books, the knowledge buried between their covers, and the teachers' guidance, but my reasons were far from hers. I went for the painting. I loved its size, its flush of dyes, and the kaleidoscopic loudness. More so, I went for the glee the parade of multicolored shops sparked in me, for the lightness it created in my chest, and for the excitement that thrummed through my body. But mainly, I went because Howsen's Bakery and Sweets shop was on the way.

My shoulders sagged. The size of the crowd collected outside the left window of the principal attraction had multiplied from that of yesterday. The boys had chased the girls away, and the ninnies had not bothered to linger for a second chance. Why would they? The boys were brash and impatient, and the girls were brittle beings.

I hopped across the road disfigured by ruts carrying water down-hill, scars imprinted in the rain-soaked ground by the wagons and cabs' wheels. According to the northerners, their narrow bodies on slender wheels tugged by trim horses couldn't be responsible for the damaged gravel road. They said it was impossible, inconceivable; they were made scapegoats when the southern Bisamburi's habit of overloading wagons was the real problem. But the truth was the truth.

"Our transport rides on air," one of my neighbors often said in a mocking voice and with exaggerated haughtiness. "Its body is as airy as a feather. And the horse is light as whipped cream. How could my cab do any damage?" Our convulsive laughter followed. It was difficult not to indulge, especially when the impersonator was so witty and comical and high society was the subject.

Ahead, the boys buzzed like a swarm of bees against the large left win-dow, hovering and shifting in quick, clipped motions. Their height nor their gender would deter me. I abandoned my books and pencils at the adjoining candle-maker's storefront and sauntered to the group. Soon after, I grunted and poked my elbow into the waist of the red-hatted boy, then buried my kneecap into the back of the knee of someone else and tugged on another classmate's collar to drag him out of the way. In the end, I bent and squeezed in between two pairs of scrawny legs to secure my favorite spot where the tallest jars were placed and where the window fogged the least.

I breathed in the splendor: the reds, and the blues and the pinks and the purples; rounds and squares and rectangles and triangles along with other shapes that couldn't have ever wriggled into my imagination, had it not been for the creator.

Jaja Howsen was a northerner. But I didn't bother with trifles because the real marvel was his talent for conceiving dramas of wonder. Yes, it superseded the painter's work hanging in Mercy Terrace. Yes, even the newspapermen had recognized his skill.

With art supplies of candies and jellies, he created a different picture each morning—original and extraordinary. He spelled words and drew pictures and made flower arrangements with them, made the sugar pearls seesaw from one bowl to the other every few minutes, and even hung confections from the ceiling.

I often wondered how long a single display—a play in a theater, really—took to plan and implement. With those details, drawing a picture of a tree alone, coloring aside, would occupy me for a fortnight. And where did he sandwich the hours involved in the making of the sweets?

This morning my eyes fastened on a clear vase. Lumps of yellow rolled in pink sugar adhered to a short, white stick. The shade of the gob of yellow seemed so unusual, so eye-catching, I presumed the flavor had to be unique. Saliva gathered in my cheeks' pockets. Jaja Howsen must have gotten the ingredients from outside of Bisamburi. Perhaps he had sailed to the nearby continent of Terra One, crossed the vast expanse of the land to get to the changing city of Ashmere. Or maybe he'd voyaged to Yelyern or Lyehell on the other continent. Except Jaja Howsen didn't look like he had seen any other place apart from our island of Oal.

"Get out of my way, Sukhi," Devan, my neighbor's eldest son, said.

I pressed my fingers on the ledge and flattened my nose against the glass. Jaja Howsen added a plate of green square jellies, the color of tender grass. They promised a long-lasting effect in my mouth, but since green was the worst color ever to exist and I despised chewing grass, I decided I wouldn't choose them; that was, if I was given a choice. The dream of selecting a confection, gauging its weight in my hand, and catching its whiff before gulping it was mouthwatering. It was also an illusion. But who could blame me for fantasizing?

"Move over, Devan," someone said. "You've had enough."

"Sukhi's the one who should back out," another said.

I wasn't interested in the jostle and the petty quarrel surrounding me. The boys always argued, wrestled, and got themselves in trouble.

Instead, I was lost, yearning for the pink on the yellow. The sugar was crystalline and multifaceted, resembling rosy gems peeking out of silk headscarves, studding the earlobes of the ladies whose plump purses were strung around their waistlines.

How much force would my jaws need to grind those crystals to a paste? How long would it take the paste to glaze the lining of my mouth, to release the pleasure locked inside until a thrill ran in circles within me? Or would it be better to savor it? Let it linger on the tongue until it stuck to it, releasing its juices as the saliva wrapped around it and pared it down, layer by layer, the item getting smaller and smaller until it vanished? Oh, what control it would require. But the bliss would prevail for hours, making it worthwhile, particularly if I didn't rinse and waited to ingest food or water, as Devan often suggested. He regarded sucking and not chewing as a far superior option to enjoy Jaja Howsen's candies.

Speaking of Devan, I found him bearing down on me, his eyes demanding me to vacate my spot. In response, I nuzzled the wall and lifted my chin at the seesawing pearls. Next I knew, he raised his leg and stomped on my shoe. In shock and pain, I squinted at my foot. It made me spin so fast that Devan froze.

He had to wreck my shoe? Ruin my single pair? The same whose straps flapped with each footstep, the broken buckles clinking with the swing and thud of footfall. Their soles were thinner than the slice of yelk meat Mother had served for breakfast, and one of them had two stitches unraveling at the back. But I made do with them. I never complained, never demanded another pair. Instead, before bedtime with Father's brushes, I worked on them, applying and reapplying the polish Mother had bartered for, rubbing in circles, polishing and buffing the leather until they reflected the light from the candles and the lantern. And I'd taken care walking this morning, avoiding the mucky gravel since the rain had pitter-pattered half the night. But all my efforts had been for naught.

I blinked at him, my lips set in a grim line.

He backed out of the throng, and I followed him.

"Look, Jaja Howsen brought out a new tray," Devan said, pointing. "Look."

Devan was known for his impulsiveness, trouble-making, and slick ways of wriggling out of situations. Rather than be tricked, I returned the favor with more force than he'd landed on my toes. He yowled. The pack mollified. Jaja Howsen stirred within his shop.

"It's not fair, Sukhi." Devan squatted on the dirt to pamper his foot. "Mine was an accident."

"Next time you do this, I'll *take* your shoes until your mother buys me a pair."

Jaja Howsen stepped outside his door, his paunch leading the way. The crowd dispersed. People, his folk from the north mainly, labeled him as the best-dressed man in Bisamburi. His starched shirts were overlaid with embroidered vests, and he paired them with trousers which seemed to live permanently underneath an iron, but at present, bearing a sour expression and a stick in his hand, he didn't look so dandy.

In a not-so-distant past, he'd dwelled in constant fury and yelled at the children loitering by his store window. Mother had mentioned his father being the same during her childhood. But of late, Jaja Howsen had grown crafty. He tied the bell on his shop door before coming out unannounced with a stick, and the inattentive received his not-so-sweet treatment.

"How could he be so mean to his customers?" I'd asked Mother one day, and she clarified we weren't his patrons. She was right. I'd yet to see my classmates or neighbors buy any treats from his store. Although on occasion I *had* seen, behind the left window, finely dressed ladies studying and tasting his goods and exiting with bulging brown bags and wide smiles washed in lustrous lip color.

It wasn't that Mother and I had never set foot inside. We bought bread from him on special occasions, but the important part was I'd never ventured in the left half, the candy half of the store. Extra pennies were hard to earn. Mother said money was too precious to be spent on frivolous items that didn't last longer than baby Jovan's coughing fits, despite the promise of intense delight.

"Scram, you begging dullards! You good-for-nothings! Your kind needs a good walloping." Jaja Howsen's bald head shone as bright as the sun rising behind him. It took courage to bare one's head, and few dared in Bisamburi; in fact, our entire island of Oal covered their heads per Mother. Was he applying a tincture or some medicinal oil to grow his hair? Not obtained from Saaja, our medicine woman, Goddesses forgive, because she was beneath him, a pure quack, but from a doctor from his locality, prestigious and official.

Upon hearing the threat behind him, Devan snapped upright—he dared not show his face to the shopkeeper. Nonetheless, he stomped his foot with force in a puddle of muddied water between us and tore at my headscarf. Then, with his hands in his pockets and a smirk on his face, he took flight.

I swayed forward at the force of his effort, my scarf dragging halfway down my scalp. I gasped. With swift thinking and the quick motion of my hands, I repositioned the scarf, hiding the spread of midnight black veiling my head.

But I was a breath too late. Jaja Howsen's glare twisted into scrutiny and his belligerent demeanor transformed into one of shock. The stick fell from his hands. He'd glimpsed what he wasn't supposed to—a secret Mother and I had concealed, disguised, and protected since my birth.

"No!" I whispered, trying to blink away the dirt of the puddle Devan had splattered in my eyes.

My hands shook, and I stumbled, forgetting the tussle with Devan, forgetting my shoes, and I squeezed my eyes shut, replaying the scene my mother had repeatedly warned me against.

"I wasn't supposed to . . ." Dread expanded in my core. The grit scraped my eyes under the pinched lids.

Even Father was ignorant of my being born with hair. That was the way of Oal. Only mothers and midwives knew the character of the heads of the babies, except in some circumstances. And they never divulged.

"No, it didn't happen. It didn't happen. It didn't—"

What had I done? Oh, dear Goddesses, what had I done?

I turned away. I'd broken something, something monumental, considerably more important than the forbidden exposure. Something I didn't think I could reverse, but what was it? The coils of my bowels felt knotted behind my belly button, and my breath, confused and strangled, gave me the notion that my lungs had crisscrossed in my chest—a horridness that I knew wouldn't disappear soon. Where would I go in the meantime? Home, to bury my misery in my pillow? I shook my head. Mother was the last person I wanted to encounter.

Head down, I scurried away from the confectioner, one hand pressed over my scarf and the other over my chest. As I held my breakfast down with clenched jaw and jagged breath, I wished Jaja Howsen's chimney would stop discharging the cloying, nausea-arousing odor.

I lumbered along Burned Mill Road, alone and unsmiling, toward my school, throwing nervous glances over my shoulder, no longer bothered by the puddles, my books and pencils forgotten by the candle maker's.

Upon reaching there, I feigned composure.

A sigh escaped from me when the last bell ended the school day, my upper back aching from holding my shoulders tight through the hours.

The pretend calmness I'd worn as a badge of bravery had deserted me half an hour into my school day, and from then on, my unease had worsened. My mind alternated between on and off the entire day. Of the scads of words Jeje Anana scribbled with her energetic hand on the chalkboard, a scattering was all I remembered. During lunch, my friends clenched my arm and dragged me into their conversations time and time again, but somehow staring at the smattering of light glittering through the overarching crown of the tree we sat under was more pacifying. I retained little of their conversation. And Jaja Tasser's lessons were a complete blur. Then there was the repeated chiding from my teachers for having forgotten my school supplies. After a while, seeing it made no difference to me, they ceased.

The insides of my abdomen still played jump rope as I trudged across the school compound, but the feeling that the sky or the earth would crack open any minute and monsters would seize me had abated.

I had gathered enough courage to return home. My plan was to bury myself within a horde of children and to keep my eyes on the road, by my feet, nowhere else. Then go straight to my cot. I would curl up facing the wall with a book over my face to make Mother think I was studying. I craved to be left alone.

"Sukhi, how did you get mud on your dress?" Mother fed Jovan, who kept crawling away from her after each spoonful of oat porridge. "You know how hard it is for me to get the marks out."

One glance around the room told me father wasn't home.

"I know you're going to nag me again about wearing my pinafore." Taking my shoes off, I flung myself on the covers and hid my face. Thirteen-year-olds didn't parade around like babies wearing pinafores over their dresses.

"What's the matter?" Mother sat at the edge of my cot, determined not to leave me alone.

She would mince me if I told her about Jaja Howsen being privy to our secret.

"If you say I'm so special for having hair, why do we have to hide it?" I allowed the resentment and indignation in my tone to rise. "Do you think people will harass me for having hair?" After all, the scariest person I knew had done nothing except gape.

Mother was silent for so long that I became curious and shifted to observe her. She watched Jovan. His lips were encircled with cream paste, a stark contrast to his fitted black cap covering his head. Did he have hair? I could have stolen a peek any time, but it was indecent, obscene even, to break the norm of privacy with that kind of sneaky intention. It would be like undressing someone because one was curious about the other's private parts. Residents of Oal shunned such behavior.

The dimple on Jovan's cheek depressed deeper as he made noises while shunting his toy boat back and forth on the floor. When he suspected our attention on him, he veered his large eyes at us, babbling about the details of his play, happy in his one-sided conversation. Jovan *was* adorable. I glanced at Mother again. No, Mother wasn't studying my brother. Her stare was distant and empty. She was doing what I had done in school.

After a while, she said in a subdued voice, "It's time to tell you why you are special. And why you have to conceal it. But you have to make a promise to me. Will you?"

"It's my hair that makes me special." My stomach had calmed in Mother's presence. "But how can you be sure other girls don't have hair if everyone in Bisamburi walks around with scarves? They might all be special."

Mother removed my scarf and stroked my strands, the front part of which she dyed for me to match the brown of the skin of my forehead, the brown of the rest of me, in case my scarf ever slipped a bit. However, a bit was not what had been exposed. A bit was not what Jaja Howsen had seen.

Mother's posture was slumped. Wetness and dullness filled her eyes. "There is much more I haven't told you."

"Like what?"

"I want you to agree you'll keep this tucked away in a far corner of your heart. It's for you to know and none other. Just like the knowledge about your hair. And also never to use your hair for frivolous purposes."

The morning's scuffle with Devan, and Jaja Howsen's change in demeanor swam to the forefront of my mind. My guts conducted themselves the way they had earlier at school.

"I will," I said, except her last sentence made no sense.

"Your father . . . he doesn't work."

"I know."

"And repairing clothes . . . also, the number of ropes I'm able to make per day for the merchandiser . . . what I earn through those two is—scant but suffices for the four of us. The landlord, the food, candles or oil for the lanterns, the clothes, and other necessities are managed, but not much else. Do you understand what I'm saying?"

I nodded. Father drank friss from glass bottles throughout the day, a drink that angered him and made him shout mean words and falsehoods. It was funny how he could slide into a doze anytime and anywhere, his yawn frozen, the pink of his tongue and palate and cheeks visible for hours, and his arms so floppy I could make shapes with them—like the balloon man with his long, slender balloons—and entertain Jovan. But my antics never amused Mother.

"I'm sorry to burden you with this, but it's time you knew," Mother said. "How do you think we pay for additional expenses?"

"By saving and sacrificing?" I recalled how I curbed my desires for Jaja Howsen's confections, avoided waste with everything, and protected my shoes.

"Yes, but we also have another source." Mother ran her fingers through my dark locks. "These are not ordinary, Sukhi. They have the power to heal."

I flinched, then examining my hair, I said, "Are you sure?"

She caressed my cheeks. "They are magical, dear. Three to seven strands pulled from the roots, when worn around someone's neck, rid them of their sickness."

"But the medicine woman? The doctor?"

"There are some diseases which have no cure."

I knew that.

"Cleva's lameness was hopeless," she said. "Until your hair cured your friend."

My eyes gleamed, and I squealed. A heap of magic grew on my head. "Then why keep it secret? Let's give it to everyone who's sick and make them better."

She sighed. "The situation isn't straightforward. Why do you think everyone keeps their head covered? Of course, there are some shameless men who don't."

Much like Jaja Howsen . . . and father.

She continued, "Hair gives you power and wealth over others. If people learn your secret, they'll exploit you. The few times I've plucked your strands, I've done so with your permission and with a plan to barter. Not for your father's friss, but to keep us alive. Majority of the times, though, I collect the few strands you shed or those caught in your brush."

"So, you gave our secret away when you gave them my hair?"

Mother looked away from me for a few breaths before speaking. "They receive the hair on a condition that if they expose us, I seize their locket, causing the malady or disability to reappear. *I* collect information on who is sick and beyond help from Saaja, and on those who are begging for help for their own or their dearest's recovery. *I* ascertain whether it'll be a safe arrangement before approaching the person or their family. It's not the other way around. And I do it infrequently. But, most importantly, I never mention you as the source."

"So then why don't we barter more often? I have a large quantity on my head. We don't have to be so poor." I remembered a handful of times she'd taken my hair.

She gave a broken smile. "Because you don't regrow what is plucked. You might have a long life to live. And who knows what kind of life."

Jaja Howsen's behavior altered after Revelation Day—the day the baker-confectioner and I had an unexpected education about the pile under my scarf. My fear of him receded after three weeks or so, and I rejoined the boys in admiring his exhibitions. The fact was, I couldn't shun his store. The sweetmeats were an incredible lure.

He never failed to track me in the crowd at his window, nor whenever I passed by his shop. He noticed what item I salivated over and positioned it before my favorite spot. Grander and more varied and displays became the norm. The boys were bewildered when a grin appeared on his countenance. However, I knew it wasn't for them.

One day, when Mother sent me to the apothecary for some medicinal herbs, I noticed Jaja Howsen painting his storefront. I ignored him. On my way back, though, he beckoned me in his wordless way. I jammed my hands in my pockets and shrank into myself. He continued. His attempt at communicating with me—one of the unwelcomed children who loitered at his window—seemed unnatural and frightful since his disagreeable mood had been his second skin.

I kept my eyes on the road, but Jaja Howsen, fraught with wild energy, gestured whenever I peeped, animated in his behavior, wishing me to join him. He was a strange man. What had come over him? He'd never beamed so much as long as I'd known him and never bounced so much, flushed in the face with crimson. I was afraid he would break into a run, shouting at the top of his voice any moment now, following me home. Imagine the sight of that.

Yet his enthusiasm was infectious. It made me waver in my decision. The saltiness of the sea hung in the air, heavy, reminding me of my single trip to the shore: black-backed sea dibbis flying low over the white foam and hot sands, shrieking in chorus. Underneath the hint of salt, however, a milder but unyielding fragrance of lavender and roses flowed. I knew its origination. I took a few steps his way.

Halfway across the road, I hesitated. What trouble would Jaja Howsen get me into? At least it was a busy morning on Burned Mill Road, and the shops were awash with buyers. I summoned enough courage and drew near the confectionery, my frame rigid with caution.

What was he planning to do?

What he actually did was open the door for me and hold it, the bell at the doorknob ringing a jingle. I gladdened. Was this how princesses were treated? Aromas of warm bread and cakes, along with those of sugarplums, gushed out. There was no reason for alarm because his punishing stick was nowhere in sight. Besides, he grinned at me. The missing teeth didn't matter, and neither did the dried-autumn-leaves' shade of the remaining ones as long as the warmth sprang from his face.

Delight made me giddy, so much so that the foul-smelling paint fumes became insignificant. How could I stop my feet from climbing the three small steps I had scaled before to get to an area I had dreamed of but had never visited?

A mixture of wood smoke and butter emanating from Jaja Howsen's clothing got lost when a blast of syrupy goodness gave me a shocking welcome on the landing. My nose carried me to the left half of the shop. I saw what he viewed every day: the display window where my schoolmates and I crowded around and where he arranged the exquisite bites; the counter he sometimes sat behind collecting payments; the long wooden table holding surplus provisions between the two; and the low-hanging ceiling with hooks.

I spun around before I walked through the area, my eyes gluing to every item I examined. I had to remember to blink. The colors and smells, their intensity, pounced on me from every direction and cornered me, and I reveled in them with an open heart, as Father did when he brought the bottle's rim to his lip. While I was ignorant of the noises I might have produced, embarrassing though they would be, I didn't care because delicious distractions abounded and my emotions ran high.

To make the event extra-special, Jaja Howsen arranged his specialties in an S on a platter lined with a gold doily and offered it to me. A tingling surge started in my chest and spread outward through my limbs and face, and I shivered in pleasure. I couldn't wait to tell the boys. Devan would curdle and wear a shade of a color I detested, but it would suit him.

The confectioner slid the platter closer to me. As I inched my fingers to grab the stick with the pink-sugared yellow lump, I hesitated. I had no money.

"It's called a lolly." His voice was hoarse, I assumed, from the constant insults he'd shouted at the children for years. "You can have it. You don't have to pay. See, this white stick here is made of paper wound tightly on itself. And the flavor is exquisite! It was my idea. The flavor of an ordinary lemon mixed with that of a fruit called pineapple. What a genius conception! I should win an award for it." He made a hasty drawing of the strange-sounding fruit.

To me, the picture was comparable to a fountain rather than an apple. How it appeared, however, didn't matter. What mattered was the explosion of sweet and sour on my tongue the instant I drove it in. Saliva squirted out of my mouth when I opened my lips to rotate the lolly. I sucked on the confection hungrily and ground the granulated sugar between my back teeth, the crunching blending with the slurping, music I had never heard until then. The man talked to me, smiled, but my mind didn't have room for anything except the prize within the confines of my jaws. It was merrymaking of the best kind, and I wallowed in it. Gumminess stuck to my teeth and my fingers, and I rejoiced in it.

Later that night, I dreamed of lands lush with plants growing lollies in place of flowers and rain of hard round candies and air as sweet as spun pink sugar.

M other hadn't plucked my strands in a long time, so when Jaja Howsen wasn't willing to offer me his specialties except for the green jellied squares, I entertained the idea of bartering my hair for the treats. I had so many. Surely she wouldn't miss any.

"Do you know of anyone who has hair?" Acknowledging the unspoken secret between us rumpled my composure.

"You," Jaja Howsen said.

"Anyone besides me?"

"No."

"Since—since I don't have any money, would you accept—accept my . . .?"

A hint of hunger flashed in his ordinary black eyes between blinks, but I could be mistaken.

"What would I do with it?" He cocked his head and tapped his finger on his chin. "But since you insist, I'll take it as payment. I cannot deprive a little girl of what she loves best."

The quickness of his acceptance was awkward. His pause seemed forced, inconsistent with the eagerness he had shown since he had located me outside. Yet I was flooded with an odd sense of relief. I sagged against the center table. With the tension released, the urge to share the magical aspect of my valued possession burned through me. But Mother's words and my promise to her resurfaced, and my breath quickened. I wasn't supposed to share my bounty in such haste, dispense it with such imprudence, in particular since he called me "a little girl." I clenched my teeth.

Jaja Howsen locked the front door before going into the backroom to fetch a mirror. A strange feeling overcame me. Vestiges of the sickness of Revelation Day came charging back. The brown scarf had never come off in another's presence except Mother's. My promise to her haunted me.

"Can I bring it with me tomorrow?" I said.

"But the best toothsome tasties will be gone by then," he said.

My heart galloped, and I swallowed hard several times to suppress the shrinking feeling in my chest. Oh, how difficult it was. I knew, however, I couldn't have it both ways. I was almost a woman now, and a courageous woman was adaptable and made hard decisions with ease, like Mother.

Much to my annoyance, Jaja Howsen wouldn't settle for a number less than fifteen for five pieces of sweetmeats.

"But that is too high a price."

"Nowhere near their value in anes." He picked off a few price cards and showed them to me.

My ignorance of the cost of items made me lean in, somewhat curious but mostly to pretend worldliness and to appease him. Except the price blew my unruffled indifference to shreds. The neat writing surrounded by flourishes indicated not a handful of copper anes as I was sure but silver ones. I stifled a gasp and took a step back. No one in my section could afford them. No wonder Mother denied indulging my desires, her intent stemming from monetary incapacity and not, as I had long convinced myself, from her spite.

I agreed to his asking fee.

He waited, his eyes switching between my hands and my scarf, his wolfish attention unnerving. So, I requested privacy, and the shopkeeper proposed his storage room. There, with shaky hands, I untied the two braids Mother had woven and overlapped in a spiral and harvested the amount he wanted. In return, he handed me five candies of my selection wrapped in waxed paper and secured with a satin ribbon.

From then on, I refused to let Mother tie my locks. My head felt lighter, I told her, without the taut twists and braids squeezing it like a vise. When my response to her concern for my casually secured locks tumbling out didn't satisfy her, she spouted a sermon on the scarf as a second line of security and said that my newly adopted loose-fitting style would not guard against heavy, wayward hair. She quibbled, and I declared it was secure enough. Besides, she needn't know about the various colored ribbons—acquired in my transactions—that fastened and adorned my hair.

Still, she continued to shoot many looks and words of disapproval, day after day after day. Finally, when I couldn't bear her complaints anymore, I proclaimed I'd matured and wanted to make my own decisions. Mother had no argument left in her.

Over several months, I became the confectionery's regular visitor. I was careful to distribute the hair collection to make it less noticeable. But as time passed, Jaja Howsen raised the price of his sweetmeats from fifteen strands for five pieces to fifteen for three.

My scalp became more and more visible with each passing day.

M other came and sat next to me as I combed my locks, preparing for school. Father was elsewhere. Lately, he preferred the nearest runnelhouse to guzzle friss because she had raised a tempest a few weeks ago on account of Jovan. My brother had gotten to his bottle and poured it over his head. The inky liquid and the foam skimming it streamed into the openings of his face, the sting rendering him inconsolable for two days. When his arms and legs flopped and his head lolled akin to Father's, she uttered silent curses among her prayers.

"What is friss made of?" I had asked.

"Nothing good," she had replied, but Father said, "It's made of harmless, common items. Fermented fruit like Jambu-berry. Maize, pitatan roots, and tobacco."

On that occasion, I believed Mother. Not because friss stank up our home, but because Jovan's distress and the similarity of his behavior to Father's when he drank too much unsettled me. Anyway, since then, the house was neater without the strewn empty bottles and more spacious without the cases of his full ones.

"What is happening to your hair?" Mother asked. "It seems less lush."

"Nothing." I picked up my scarf and draped it around my head in careless folds.

"Do you feel well?" She took my chin in her hand.

"You don't have to worry about me."

"You talk in a strange way . . . open wide."

I didn't.

"You've lost your teeth, haven't you? How many?"

Five, but I wasn't the first person in Bisamburi to do so.

"Do you remember the promise you made to me, Sukhi?"

I stared at the brush in my hand. My given promise felt meaningless.

"I want the best for you. I hope you are making thoughtful decisions," Mother said. When I didn't reply, she hardened her voice. "I don't want you to stop anywhere on your way to and from school."

I looked into her eyes and found harshness.

"Including the confectioner's."

What unpleasantness, I thought and averted my eyes from her.

As winter turned to spring, the shape of my scalp emerged. It was neither round like Jaja Howsen's nor lumpy like Father's—it was lopsided. Also, food was harder to chew.

I ignored Mother's repeated warnings until one day, she banned me from going outdoors altogether. She lodged by the door during the day, abandoning most of her duties, and slept there at night. She even dragged the baby's crib there. When she found me eyeing the window, she nailed wooden boards—which she got by prying apart a shelf—across the two windows of our home, leaving openings wide enough for sunlight and air to pass but narrow enough to stall me from nurturing any grand ideas.

In response to the change, Father's moods worsened, and his words became sharper, like claws digging into Mother's skin. Jovan fretted and issued more crying spells than she could soothe.

One morning, as I lay stretched on my bed, I observed Mother rocking my brother in her arms by the tender light. Her resolve appealed to me less and less each day, and I realized I'd come to a point where her stiff back, the frequent hand gesturing, and the stern looks had become detestable.

Jovan couldn't be soothed into sleep during the dark hours. She searched for water in the vessel on the stove, the clay water-storage pot beside it, and the buckets, one by the door and the other in the chaukdi outside—amid clangs and knocks and the "no" and the "it can't be." Then she glanced helplessly around. Father, meanwhile, snored in spurts.

"Sukhi, tend to Jovan until I get water from Devan's mother."

The chaukdi was a stone-tiled square, sunken a step, around which we could pull a curtain if needed, and in whose corner opened a drain to remove dirty water from our washing. Above, a quarter way from the bottom, jutted a tap. The city released water for an hour at four in the afternoon. It was a hectic time, a sacred time, one to be protected from other jobs without exception. But because Mother had assumed a sentry's role, she had forgotten the responsibility of filling the water pot and the buckets for our family, and now she implored me for help.

I flung my body around and faced the wall.

"He hasn't drunk enough liquids since yesterday!"

In response to my silence, she crept through the door, closing it behind her. The moment she departed, I rose and followed, ignoring my brother's whimpers, waited by the door, and counted to ten before pulling the handle. Contrary to my suspicion, the door was unlocked.

Freedom at last!

I scampered through the streets toward Burned Mill Road, away from Devan's home, away from my prison, basking in the soft glory of the rising sun and the fading haze. The sparrows partook in my cheer and my springy steps. It was a Thursday morning, quite early for school and shops to open, but fellow travelers had tasks to accomplish. I acknowledged them and didn't care if they remained aloof or returned an inquiring or a reproachful look. What mattered was that Mother's stranglehold was gone. And with it the confinement within those gray, gloomy walls. Liberty had never tasted so wonderful.

To my shock, Jaja Howsen approached me.

"I wondered where you had disappeared," he said, his head covered in a hat, which made him unrecognizable and appear wider.

Why was he visiting my neighborhood?

"Were you growing tired of the selection I served you?"

I readied to deny his allegation and spill the truth about my mother and my imprisonment but stopped.

"I was afraid I would never see you again," he said, reminding me of the ugliness of his voice.

I chewed my lip and rubbed my forehead. It was me who sought his shop and his goods and not the reverse.

"So, I brought you items you have never laid eyes on." He inverted his hat and, reaching in, brought out a brown paper bag. He dangled it at my nose before laying it across his hand and forearm. Then, at a turtle's pace, he set to tearing the paper along one side, my craving leaping, my patience wilting.

When he finished, shiny brown balls rested on the paper in his palm, the most odious-looking edibles I'd ever seen. They appeared to be more suitable coming out of the rear end of the horses on the side of the road than being put in one's mouth. But the whiff of deliciousness discharging from it was more than pleasing.

"Go on, try it. It has softened from the heat of my body."

When I tried to pinch off a piece from one of them for taste, he said, "No, ingest the whole ball."

I did. And as I was about to crush it to a pulp, its shell melted, and flavors of flowers and cream and sugar surfaced. No candy was so smooth on my tongue nor underwent so dramatic a change within moments, and the hints of surprising bitterness . . . I looked at him with widened, smiling eyes because my brain had forgotten how to form words. Also, my mouth was packed.

"It's called chocolate." He extended his hand an extra inch. "I made them for you."

If I was in paradise before with his other lollies, I was in Upper Realm with the ones in his palm. I devoured the second.

"You approve of them."

I nodded, swirling the brown paste around. But the instant I went to snatch a third, Jaja Howsen withdrew his offering.

"Remember our deal?"

"Fifteen."

"Fifteen?" He chuckled. "No, my dear girl, this has cost me a fortune. Fifteen won't do."

"Oh?"

He opened his mouth to speak and shut it. "I won't part with these for anything less than all," he said in a frank manner.

"All?" I didn't understand. "All what?"

"*All* of your hair."

I recoiled. All meant living with naught. All meant no brushing, no washing, and it also meant no softness around my face at night as I rested against the pillow. It implied no warmth in winter. It suggested being bald and ordinary like Father—like the man before me—for the rest of my life.

"I can give you a better value. What if I give you a second bag of chocolates?" He pulled out another bag from his hat, equaling a magician performing his trick with a young, meek vicot, wings thick with pink down and startled eyes.

Jaja Howsen never ceased to amaze me.

"Better yet, I'll give you three bags. Because I'm a generous man." He opened my hand. "Here, try two more pieces."

I rammed them in lest he retracted his offer, my cheeks resembling a bloated blowfish, my lips unable to connect. The warm, melted liquid dribbled from the corners of my lips. How could I refuse such ambrosial sweetness? How could anybody?

So, I snuck in the narrow passageway in between two houses, away from his curious, shameless stare, where the tight space contained nothing more than the open gutter meant to drain rainwater away to Lake Lerling. And straddling this channel of foul stagnant puddles, shoes sinking into the mossy ground, I plucked the payment for Jaja Howsen's rare delicacies.

"How do I know you gave me the complete amount?" he said when I handed him the remnants, which he pocketed.

"But—but I have."

He didn't demand to view my scalp; he didn't put forth a suggestion of wanting to do so; he just held out his bags and swayed them under my nose.

At the side of the busy road, with trembling fingers, I undressed my head in broad daylight. Stern remarks, harsh glares, and interruptions by charitable people didn't prevent his scrutiny nor his request for me to twirl as he ensured I was a truth-teller.

Once the scarf was repositioned and the bags were in my hands, the people stood by me to watch him leave. The whole time, I couldn't bear the wait. To think of sharing was unreasonable. Whether Jaja Howsen had given me an excellent bargain or not, I had paid a massive amount; therefore, they were mine, every last morsel.

I returned to the secluded space and gorged on them.

When I returned home, scraping the chocolate off my cheeks, chin, and neck with my fingernails and licking them clean, Mother stood at the threshold, waiting, cradling Jovan. His head leaned against her chest as he sucked his thumb, listless.

"Where were you?"

I attempted to squeeze between her and the door frame. She swung and caught me with one arm. Deprived of support in her movement, Jovan's head drooped away from her chest, his slackened neck angled at an unnatural slant. He made no effort to correct it.

"What's on your face?" she said.

"Mud."

"Mud doesn't smell swee—"

"What do you want, *Mother*? Do you want to know if I ate what you forbade? No, I didn't eat those."

Her shoulders loosened.

"I ate a treat *far* better than you can suppose." I flung my scarf on my cot and smiled. "And I have no regrets. None."

She flashed an alarmed look in the room's corner, but only nasal whistles arose from Father's lax form. She glanced from my face to my scarf and then to my scalp. Head shaking and lips trembling, she stretched her hand backward for support from the table, eyes fixated on my scalp's bareness. Then, as if a sudden horror had gripped her, her features warped into an emotion I had never seen, and her throat emitted a thick aching groan I had never heard. And under the strain of that horror, her knees buckled, and she dropped to the floor. The thud aroused friss-soaked Father, who muttered a few words with half-opened, vacant eyes.

My attention, however, was riveted on Jovan nestled in Mother's arm. No injury had come to him, being cushioned by her body, but the fall should have startled him, made him cry, blare as he sometimes did, or, at the least, caused him to pick himself up and crawl to safety. Instead, he lay as he had landed. He stared at the ceiling, the fixedness aimless in its purpose, his doll-like body sluggish. A single change was induced: the vigor with which he sucked his thumb.

Jovan's behavior was so peculiar, it withered my vexation. An empty feeling rose in the pit of my stomach and my hands . . . I didn't know what to do with them. I nipped fragments off my nails, but when it didn't pacify me, I shook them and then buried them in my armpits. Nothing reassured me.

Sunlight streamed through the open door, fervent and hot across the floor. I walked to it. Outside was bright, and the sky brimmed with clouds, light and white against the vast blueness, content and pushing east, fluid in their motion. Our lane was alive, workday hubbub stirring the air. Southerners carried on with their day, coming and going, carrying buckets and bulging bags and packages. Two nearby residents chatted as they swept the dirt off their open veranda while a few of my friends strolled home from school for lunch, head-to-head, conferring secrets, sharing giggles and whispers, and occasionally letting out outbursts of emotion.

I raised my foot to step out, but my strength somehow drained. Fleeing twice was wrong. A squelch from Jovan made me spin.

What had Mother been engrossed in before I'd fled the first time?

Water.

The bucket stood beside the door, dented with age, half-full, and the drinking glass in its shadow. Mother's face was serene, devoid of emotions and lines, and it refreshed my memory of the clear blue outside. The tranquility seemed more unnatural the longer I studied her. Where was the smile she retained in her sleep, and the smattering of frowns? Without them, her face felt empty, drab, as if the colors had been sucked out of Burned Mill Road, altering it into a dull row of grays and browns.

Kneeling aside them, I drizzled water on their faces, which I followed up with blasting glassfuls when it brought no change. Jovan remained as before, aside from a brief enlivening of his eyes and a pause before he gulped in air. Mother didn't stir.

What was wrong with him? I nudged him, gentle at first, followed by a vigorous joggle. The thumb fell out of his mouth, and after a smack, he closed his lips. No other movement occurred except for the slow blinking. I broke out in a cold sweat. What had I done?

"Jovan!" I said. "Mother, wake up. Father!"

The interior was noiseless as the classrooms of my school when shut up for the rainy season.

What should I do? I scanned the vicinity of our home, my eyes stalling at my scarf. My hair, I should use my hair. My hand froze halfway across my scalp, and an uncontrollable shudder swept through my body.

"What—have—I . . .?"

I retreated to my cot, and curling my arms around my knees, I pulled them to my chest. My head spun, my brain ablaze, replete with images of Jaja Howsen's toffees and smiles, his shop's inner room, the twinges of hair-pulling, the aches in my jaw, the banging of Mother's hammer on the nails against the board and the resulting frights in Jovan, and the melting chocolate.

The blindfold fell off, clarity emerging. Agony burst in my chest, and I cried out.

And Jaja Howsen . . . the thought of him made me dig my nails into my skin.

And what about me? I swallowed hard. I was foolish, gullible. No, I was half-witted and laughable. How had he described me? "A little girl." Precisely the type who needed to wear a pinafore. I was greedy and selfish. What a monstrous folly my shortsightedness had been. My cheeks burned. I wanted Jovan's affliction transferred to me. I wished for death.

Would Jovan die if I idled?

A frenzy seized me. I rummaged through my bedding, pulling the cover off the pillow and shaking it along with the blanket, disrobing the mattress, raking my hands through its lumps and bumps. I felt like a sailor adrift in the storm, looking for our island of Oal, his ship groaning, sails whipping, metal clanking, the ever-present threat of a rollover. Worse, the possibility of a wreck.

Careful thought and method would have been better, but who would do that when their mind was captured by an urgency, building and building, a threat strong enough to swallow everything they had known? But I didn't want to think of the details or the dreadful consequences. I wanted a solution to reverse the problem.

With my body against the bottom of the far wall, I forced my breath to calm. Before me lay the continuous floor of our home, most of it lit by the door and the windows. The gloom of the corners, however, wasn't heavy enough to muddy vision. A thin coat of dust lay everywhere, spindly webs hung in nooks, and footprints were left behind from the last mopping, but no hair. Desperation wanted me to curl up within myself and remain motionless until eternity. Let the dust blanket me, undisturbed, band by band, the thickness and weight of it burying me and my turmoil, crushing me.

But what of my brother?

I couldn't abandon ship yet. I studied the wrangled bedding, the aftermath of my bout of hysteria. By the end of the cot, by its leg, lay a single serpentine length of my past.

"Yes," I said in triumph.

With a section of Mother's woven straw used for rope-making, scissors, and the newfound treasure, moments later, Joven had an ornament knotted around his neck. Yet he was unaffected.

Had the strand lost its magic? What had Mother said—three to five? No, she'd mentioned three to seven. We had one.

I noticed my hairbrush and rushed to it. There, entwined between the bristles, coiled a short strand of the night . . . such luster . . . my scanty piece of satin, my luxury, my wealth. I had been richer than the wealthiest northerner. Alas, not anymore.

Once wound on my brother's necklace, I scurried out of the house and to the other end of the lane and knocked on Cleva's door.

"Jovan's sick," I said to her mother when she stepped into the opening.

Confused, Cleva's mother asked about mine.

"She can't help him," I said. "Nobody can. Only Cleva."

"What do you mean?" She stared at my baldness. "Where is your scarf?"

"Mother's senseless on the floor, and Jovan . . ." My eyes swam.

"I'm coming with you." She reached for her outdoor shoes and grabbed the doorknob. "and cover your head, for goddesses' sake."

"No, I need Cleva." I leaned in and darted my gaze around in the inner dimness. "Cleva!"

"What are you blabbering about, child?"

Cleva ran to the commotion, her eyes wide.

"I need the hair in your locket. Hurry." My hands became agitated again. "Quick. Give it to me."

She looked at her mother, unsure.

"One," I said, my heart at a gallop. "Just one." When neither responded, I added, "I wouldn't ask if I had any other choice."

Her mother's face hardened. "We made a transaction with your mother. The exchange cannot be revoked. For Cleva's sake."

"But Jovan will—die." A wad of saliva choked me. Dizzy, I lost my balance and landed on the tiled veranda floor.

When my senses returned, I lay in a puddle of water, my shirt stuck to my chest and my head wrapped with cloth. I resumed my begging until Cleva's mother dragged her daughter and me to our home.

Mother screamed, at the heavens, at the world, at Father, at Jovan, at me. The rest of the world was absent to her, though. With no need for further explanations, Cleva's mother unlatched my friend's locket, unthreaded a single tendril, and overlapped it with the existing one around my brother's neck. I forbade my friend to sit and watched her the whole time, lest her lameness returned in consequence to the removal of a hair from her locket. It didn't.

Within minutes, Jovan, startled by Mother's shriek, let out his favorite word—boat—kicked over, and crawled to the corner where Father watched in passive dullness. Only then did Mother submit.

I rushed to Mother, ground my head into her neck, my arms around her, and sobbed. Snot and tears and drool flowed and mingled as I poured out my rambling apologies in between gasps. She didn't scold me nor blame me nor disown me. Instead, she embraced me in her softness while showering praises and gratitude to my friend and her mother.

In a flash of lucidity, a sobering thought arose: Mother didn't issue useless warnings as I had led myself to believe. On the contrary, she was the wisest woman I knew, a kind of storage pot brimming with kindness, with affection, forgiveness, and with much more I had yet to discover. Our family was nothing without her. Jovan and I would be lost without her.

She was our world.

3

— . —

A Cardinal Delusion

Javala's preoccupations began in the most innocent ways. So when she remarked the cardinal hadn't been sighted yet one midafternoon, as I stepped into the house after a long day of selling pancakes, I paid no attention to it.

Tall and lean, she stood by the window opposite the kitchen, peering out. Nothing about her or the usual mood of our place gave me any hint of the approaching whirl of restless trouble. I went about my day: stacking the ingredients bought from the grocer, shaking the pancake crumbs from the empty baskets, settling them on the wall hooks for the next day's market batch, and cleaning the kitchen of the mayhem I had left behind in the morning's haste.

When I turned to clear the table, tucked in the corner beside the window, her untouched breakfast surprised me. The egg, cheese over a slice of bread and a ripe brufruit she had sat with when I parted were dry. Her tea was cold. Yet Javala remained with a palm splayed against the pane and the other clutching a wooden cane, unbothered by hunger.

"Do you have no appetite?" I said.

If she replied, her answer was lost in the unintentional tremors she suffered without relief.

I frowned as I collected the stale food and exited to feed the stray neighborhood dog.

How I wanted to warn her that every meal not eaten was another layer of meat lost off her bones, another chance for her bones to poke further through her skin. But to express my disapproval violated some moral code in her opinion. She rebelled by calling me "bloodbug." The word meant that once I began my nagging, I didn't cease till my demands over-taxed her, till my belly was engorged with satisfaction like a bloodbug's with blood. That this habit of mine caused her leanness. As much as she believed her claim to be valid, it wasn't. And I didn't nag either. It was more like a gentle nudge.

Still, to avoid giving credence to her assertion, I had learned to bury most of my reminders regarding her food deprivation. But I never quelled my concern, never. I had promised her care to my husband on his deathbed. And even if I hadn't, I would not let her wither away.

By the time I returned, she had not altered her stance.

"Javala, I'm going to prepare for your wash."

She didn't stir or acknowledge me. Her weaker leg should hurt from standing so long.

"Javala!"

For all I knew, she might want to eat first. Goddesses knew how much my stomach was calling for the pancakes I had set aside ahead of my departure to the market. Hers might too.

"Where is he?" she said, stretching her neck.

"Who?" I bent, opened the firebox of the stove and poked at the embers.

"The cardinal, Saati, the cardinal. Who else?"

"He's probably elsewhere. Flying, looking for food." I added firewood and settled the skillet. "Will you eat virrio shoots with your pancakes?"

"Why doesn't he visit me?" Her doleful complaint thrust me out of my routine and made me stare at the thin plait starting from the back of her head, hanging past her shoulders, and brushing her waist, beautiful and uncommon black turned to appealing white. Not the color of lint my commonplace brown would change into.

Oh, bother! I glanced at the shelf on the wall above the table. Lined on it were the remnants of the lures of her past. The wood piece was long, and so was the list of items perched on it.

I sighed.

Virrio shoots had to be prepared for our supper; after supper, our soiled outfits needed washing, then hanging, and the floor needed a good sweep. Also, both of us needed a scrub. And I had yet to tally and put away today's earnings. Which task could I compromise on? But it wasn't just a question of an isolated day, was it? Gradually and steadily, she would surrender to the figment, and the enchantment would last for days, if not months.

"Javala, we should not be troubled by feathered creatures." I took the skillet off the stove. It would have to be the reserved pancakes minus the shoots. "Birds don't live by our rules or customs or desires. Leave them be." I strode to her and tugged her arm. "Come, sit by the table. I will serve you chives and dill pancakes. They sold well at the market today."

To my relief, she did. By the time the stack I withheld for us each morning for supper was consumed, I had added cheese and a cup of broth while her awareness was diverted at the window. She finished those too.

"Now, I want you to rest," I said, closing the curtains.

If I nipped the problem early and thwarted it from gathering strength and growing, we could evade unknown woes.

"Rest? What if the bird flies by?" She got up with the support of her cane. "I need to know."

My shoulders slumped. This would not be like the pursuit of the coins. At least her behavior had found extra money from nooks and crannies, however scant the amount was. Instead, this was taking the shape of the affair of the herbs.

"Stop, Javala," I said, dragging a nearby chair and placing it between her and the drapes and holding her down by her forearms. "Let me tell you about the market."

"I know what happens there," she said. "I used to sell my laces there. My lacework could put the best lacemakers of today to shame. And I used to charge a pretty penny for them too."

"The candlemakers had a row about whether the use of wax or tallow made better candles," I said to distract her. "All we needed was a lantern seller and a par-par blocks seller to lend heat to the argument. And it didn't take long for them to arrive."

The faraway look in her eyes vanished, and her awareness crashed on me as though I had sinned. She shook off my hands and said, "The day is withering away fast, and this chitter-chatter will not help, will it?"

I gaped at her. Was this the end of it? She told me to quit wasting time and address my chores. I issued silent thanks to the goddesses.

"Now, be a help and get me some writing paper and a pencil. And also the stool from the bedchamber."

"Whatever for?" I said.

She regarded me like I had sold my brain at the market along with the pancakes.

"I'm not a twenty-year-old fledgling like you anymore. My memory needs help." Javala dragged the chair she'd sat on earlier alongside the window. "How else am I going to record my observances of the cardinal?"

Day two turned to day three, and Javala's fixation garnered power and established its presence like an unwelcomed guest. We rearranged the furniture so she could sit there until sunset, staring at the sky, at the piece of grass adjoining our house, the village path bordering it, and the woods beyond. She settled with such an air of self-importance as though she was getting paid. As if she was the infamous overlord's appointed note-taker himself.

Another change she implemented was rising around the time I did—before dawn.

Now then, let's see when he shows today, she said every day as she meandered from the bedchamber to the window, at which point I intervened. Handing her the brushing powder for her teeth and hairbrush, I pointed at the jug of water and basin and insisted on her grooming. Thankfully, she followed the directions.

Although my flow had been muddled and I awoke even earlier, at least I could continue earning for us and attend to other chores once she sank into her seat. Nothing was worse than reaching the market too late and with inadequate wares. The rivalry between vendors selling different goods was fierce, and altercations common. If a merchant didn't secure a favorable spot, she had no one else to blame except herself for the paltry income for the day. But I was organized and punctual, and those virtues had served our family well.

However, Javala had now inserted a crimp in the smooth pace. At least her new passion wasn't like when she had believed that the witch of Memora had intensified the sun's rays and the herbs of the world were going to burn. She had been in extreme agitation about their frailty. So much so that she had compelled us to accompany her to caution every family in our village about the alleged curse.

My husband and I had to save stems of all the herbs I cultivated in our front garden for future propagation. We had no say. Her fear was staunch, and her insistence was intense. Sometimes, we had to bring the mature plant inside with its pot, cramping our living space. To cook with anise and parsley and mint was one thing, but a deluge of betony, feverfew, musk mellow, and others (frilly soyote being the worst) in one's living space was another.

It was summer, and the heat inside the walls was stifling. Every morning I awoke with a headache amid the constancy of the pungent air stagnating in the two areas of our home. In fits of defiance, I chanced opening the windows and doors whenever she was distracted, but it was short-lived. She was as sharp as a hawk, and upon detection of my boldness, she loosened a torrent of rebukes at me for granting the rays an entry.

Week three was different. She roused before me and, silent like a cat, settled by the window.

"Javala?" Upon finding her bed empty and cold, I ran out of the bedchamber, afraid she had pursued, with her damaged knee, the creature in the thicket.

"Oh." I halted when I found her perched at her preferred location. "How long have you been sitting there?"

"Not long," she said from the darkness of the early hours.

The usual gleam in her eye had fogged, and I was nervous to ask her about the cardinal. Believing that talking about her newfound belief wasn't beneficial anyway, I skirted the bird's name like I avoided quarrelsome people.

"At least put on a shawl," I said. "It is getting colder now. With winter approaching."

"I'm not such a milksop that I would perish at first frost."

I draped my shawl across her shoulders and then, in vain, tried to pierce the lightlessness outside. "But it is too dark to see anything."

"I have not lost my other senses . . . yet," she said.

Give me grace! Now flapping and chirping were part of the game. I rubbed the back of my neck. I would have to count the hours of her sleep.

Was she going to renounce them too, like the food? She had, in the case of the herbs—worrying the sun would change its routine to trick her.

"At least get yourself sorted first," I said, waiting to help her, but she shooed me away.

Arguing with her was a losing exercise. I wasn't quick; I could read and write but wasn't learned, nor insightful enough to win a war of words with her. Besides, she had not gotten to seventy-five—a rare achievement in our world—on dim wits and by resigning herself to what life supplied. A person didn't have different occupations to their name, such as being headteacher of a school that served several villages, in their lifetime if they didn't possess certain qualities. Sure, she had periods of outlandish ideas like the peculiar notion she pursued now, but those were rare. I scanned the shelf and the several tokens upheld by it. Maybe *rare* wasn't the correct term.

Her morning grooming would have to wait until she agreed. I occupied myself with getting the firewood for the stove from the woodshed and then fetching the water.

The schedule rearrangement didn't help. Javala refused to tend to her appearance or eat breakfast, leaving me with surplus time in which no other housework fit. Therefore, I went to the market ahead of time with my baskets topped with steaming pancakes under large napkins. For today I had added minced onions and garlic in the batter along with butter. They were the most sought-after by the patrons. They were also Javala's and my favorite. The smell wafting to my nose was maddening and made me want to dig into the basket and shove the softness into my mouth. I resisted. These were our livelihoods. Spares were waiting in the vessel by the stove for our main meal, later in the day.

As I had planned and predicted, my stock sold out by midmorning. Now I had more time to focus on Javala.

"What took you so long? Were you dawdling on your way here?" She stood at the threshold, dressed for the day with neat hair and face.

"You know that's not in my nature," I said, pleased at the change, wondering what had brought it on.

"Come, hurry. The pancakes will not fly themselves to my plate," she said. "I'm starved. I had to resist the urge to swallow them."

"Don't you want anything else with it?" Was it possible that her fascination with the cardinal was fading? It had to be.

"Don't make me wait any longer." She limped to the chair and, dragging it out, plopped down onto it.

"You are in a pleasant mood today." I hurried with our plates lest she reverse her desire.

"That's because the cardinal decided to show his face shortly after you left."

E very night I lay awake past my usual hour to wonder about the following day, designing a plan for it to be fruitful for both Javala and me. It was futile.

This morning at the market, sitting on a tree stump behind the crates displaying my baskets, I mulled over various solutions to end Javala's unsound beliefs. While getting medications from the healer was tempting, wasting money on useless remedies wasn't sound judgment anymore. Goddesses knew how many desperate attempts my husband and I had made with them. The medicines never demonstrated their purported virtues.

"What do cardinals eat?" I asked the vendor selling biscuits a few steps from me.

She glared in reply as if I had inferred her goods were inferior to my pancakes. Perhaps she hadn't heard me amid the vendors' calls and the crowd's clamor of a busy village square market.

"What do cardinals like to eat?" I sought an answer from a man selling fried potato strips to my right.

"Pests," he said as he dropped two scoopfuls of strips in the customer's basket and accepted their money.

"Pests?"

"Yes, like centipedes and surkits. Spiders. Beetles."

Beetles and spiders and surkits? I recoiled and clamped my mouth with my palm to stifle a cry. Many nightmares about them littered my childhood. I still screamed at the sight of what he called pests, regardless of my whereabouts or the company. My reaction astounded people, made them withdraw, and caused them to question my sanity. But if Javala was close, she bore my outburst in calm indifference, occasionally accompanied by eyebrow-raising and headshaking. And when she couldn't tolerate the ridiculousness anymore, she would snatch the broom and sweep off the offending creature out of my sight.

"Berries, maybe," he replied to my unsuccessful attempt at hiding my disgust.

"Where am I going to get the berries?" I furrowed my brow. "None of the vendors sell them. It's the wrong season."

He shrugged. "The woods might have some. Or try chopped apples."

Hours tramping through the woodland, searching for berries—which might or might not be growing—was a misuse of my time. I bought a few firm apples on my way home.

As I feared, Javala was unkempt and captivated by the view beyond the window. The papers on the stool were filled with notes on weather, entries related to the bird's appearances, and if he had, then when and where. Her usual writing was voluptuous and charming, like pearls. And that was how she had begun her notes. But the fifth page atop the pile revealed scribbles, as though made by a child in haste.

"I haven't seen him yet." She stressed her words.

Before I cleared the kitchen or boiled potatoes to eat with our pancakes or finished any other pressing chores, I grabbed a knife, cut the apples to pieces, small enough that a bird would find attractive, and scattered them in the grass bordering the window.

"Excellent thinking," she said and took hold of her pencil and paper.

"Eat, Javala." I placed a plate of steaming potato wedges and warmed pancakes on the stool. "What little you nibbled before bedtime yesterday wasn't enough for the entire day. And you've eaten nothing today."

"I'm keeping watch."

"Isn't your stomach growling?" I took the potato-laden fork to her lips.

"Leave me alone, bedbug!" She brushed off my hand. "This is a serious mission, requiring deep musings and concentration."

She ate nothing all day.

The following day was the same.

As I added new apple pieces to the grass daily, I left the shriveled bits alone, hoping if the fresh portions didn't entice the cardinal, perhaps the worms chewing the decaying fragments would. The thought of crawling and wiggling bodies made me shudder.

Then I put out water for the cardinals, thinking they might want a sip as they came to repose their wings in the shade, similar to me drinking my teas.

Was it even the right time for the cardinals to be around? I knew nothing about them, but I would be a fool if I sat around idle and brooding. Hours of our lives weren't meant to be squandered. Nor were they meant to be spent moping and whining.

When Javala consumed nothing but six cups of barley broth for three straight days after the two days of not eating a morsel, I considered the silly idea of tramping through the woodland for berries.

One day, after returning from selling and finishing some housework, I put on my oldest outfit and short boots. Then, with a small basket on my arm, I tore my way through the shrubs, trees, and wild rose brambles. What a foolish mistake I made! To think I could handle the wildland when I had lived my whole life on solid ground and surrounded by human-made buildings.

Getting my boots wet in a puddle was the beginning. The veins of roots tripped me, planting my face in the ground and sending the basket flying like a startled duck. Mercifully, I didn't lose my teeth. Thorns and wiry branches scratched my arms and my face. They snagged my clothes and pulled at my hair. The double braids done along the two sides of my head and pinned in a bun became undone in strands. Then my foot got caught in the muck, and it sucked at my footwear. I had never known a lifeless form could be so greedy. When I tried to pull my foot and its boot out, I thudded onto my rear and got splattered with mud. Yet the bog didn't surrender my boot.

All this and I had yet to find a berry. Oh, bother!

I lumbered on, rubbing my hands to keep my fingers warm, unwilling to be unnerved or defeated by the shadows of the trees. But for the loud chirping and whizzing of the tiny hidden creatures, it was a completely different set of circumstances. My mind created awful sequences of events, in none of which I escaped with my flesh intact. My stomach churned. Screaming into my scarf wasn't enough relief, and the prayers I offered to the Goddesses were not sufficient. Should I be pleading with Vavajod? I stumbled and tramped along the ground covered in the leaf litter of late fall, my eyes darting at the slightest noise.

Eventually, I found a shrub. My heart leaped with joy. Its berry-laden branches shot in every direction from its base like the fountain in our village square. Eager to return before sunset, I made haste in collecting the plump purple berries. They were ripe and soft. Their skin broke upon the force of plucking, spilling the color on my skin. I used caution in my approach.

By the time I loaded the basket with the berries and was ready for the next step, I couldn't make head nor tail of the surrounding area. I examined the disturbance in the leaves on the ground, but they led me astray. After many false starts and inconveniences and losing my second boot, I wound my way to the woods' perimeter.

Unbeknownst to me, a group of women and children strode along the path about the same time. As I lunged out of the shrubbery to escape it, I shocked them, causing the women to shriek. In turn, I blanched and shrank, my heart galloping from the fright. One child swooned, and the others darted. On recovering, I wanted to explain, mollify their apprehension, except I struggled to find the right words. Anyhow, they fled before I acted.

My feet hurt and bled from several cuts, and I was spent, and I wished my husband was alive to carry my short and light body to safety. I didn't have to walk far, though. Thank the gales!

While I craved a good cleaning and resting of my feet, I had to finish the errand, so I dispersed fistfuls of the collected berries around the side of our house. The basket was three-quarters empty when I heard rapping on the glass. As I frowned at the taps, Javala's finger beckoned me. She knocked harder when I ignored her. Flinging the remaining berries in one go, I entered the warmth, my wicker basket and my arms and hands purple and sticky.

"What is it?" I said.

She exploded with laughter at the sight of me; so much so, she had difficulty letting words out of her mouth.

"Javala!"

"You look like the witch of the wild woods," she said as she paused, barely able to suppress what bubbled within her. "If there is such a thing." Loud shrieks of joy burst through. "You are a patchwork of purple and cream. Like a painter's canvas. Wide strokes of purple here. Some there." Her bellowing fit resumed.

"I'm scattering the berries because the apples didn't work."

"Those . . ." She clutched her abdomen and doubled over with roaring.

I was uneasy about her losing balance and that the cane would not be enough to break her fall. Still, she'd forgotten about the cardinal, even if for a few minutes.

"What?" I bit my lip.

"Those are attenberries," she said, interrupting her mirth. "They're poisonous. Cardinals don't eat those. Get rid of them."

Oh, bother!

I aimed for the basin. "I'm going to have to wash their juice off my arms and hands."

"And your face and your neck and your hair." She chuckled.

The mirror confirmed her remark—no wonder I had given the people on the path such a scare.

"Scrub as hard as you may, but you will have to be content for a few weeks looking like a warrior covered in war paint." A bout of hilarity seized her again. "War paint," she said. "Where are your weapons, warrior?" She resumed her boisterous amusement. "Were those strewn in the sod, too?"

I watched her in amazement for a while. Then, when I realized her unceasing cheer was melting my exhaustion and the pain in my feet, I joined her in the merriment. Humor was good for one's constitution.

I couldn't say my misadventure frittered away precious time because her laughter had improved her appetite, at least for that evening.

Her cycle of forgoing food, cleanliness, and attention to the day-to-day routine renewed, and so did my search for answers. Except this time, a carpet of snow smothered our village. It had snowed daily in the past week, and the fluff in the house's shadow mounted up to my knees.

When this fuss had begun, I had assumed the shorter days of the looming winter meant lesser time by the window, but she had sprung the matter of flutter and chirps on me. Now her focus had shifted once more. She would only accept the bird's appearance by sight.

"What is it?" I asked when she beat her fist against the pane and pleaded.

She had awoken and walked straight from her bed to the chair.

"All I need is one call a day. Is that a lot to ask?"

The desperation in her tone arrested me. "What happens if the bird doesn't show up every day?"

"I grow feeble."

"It is because of the meals you forgo. Not the bird." I moved the papers from the stool to the table, and sitting opposite her, I took her hands. "Javala, you *have to* let go of your interest in the bird."

I couldn't tell if she was disagreeing by shaking her head or it was her tremors. They had worsened too. Her eyes were roving, spanning the entire scene afforded by the glass. Sitting by her was of no avail. Yet I did until it was time for me to prepare the carrot greens and tarragon for the batter.

"It is," she said, later when I crossed the threshold with buckets of well water.

"What is?"

"Every day I don't see the cardinal, I grow feeble. And it is not the lack of food. It is his absence."

Gales preserve us! The buckets' handles slipped from my hands, and the metal clunked to the floor, sloshing and spilling water.

I mulled on the problem, spinning it over and over, examining it this way and that, not just on the way to the marketplace but while selling my wares. I couldn't determine a course to undo the puzzle she kept magnifying.

However, the answer came to me when two friends discussing ribbons stopped at my stand to buy my goods. Javala wanted a flare of red, and I would give her one. The fresh snow from today would make it striking. And if I flashed them at dusk or slightly later, she wouldn't be able to tell the difference. It had to be a quick wave, though.

A stop at the weaver and several sticks from the thicket were enough to build a tool with a long handle and a crossbar to tie each ribbon's end.

By the time I circled our dwelling's posterior to creep toward the farthest angle visible from the window, the snow had long since stalled. Javala would need to press her cheek against the surface to glimpse the ribbon and mistake it for the cardinal she so keenly sought.

As I trudged through the knee-deep snowdrift, attired from head to toe in wool and using the tool's handle as a supporting stick, I thought of the bog in the forest that had stolen my footwear. If I lost my tall boots in this venture, I would have to withstand the cold in my worn-out short ones until the snow melted. A shiver made my skin feel like that of a plucked goose.

Frosts and blizzards and snowfalls were pictures of general misery to me. I was never one to admire them. Winter made my work harder and longer. Besides, the chill got to me faster than anyone I knew. If I didn't shield my toes and fingers, the frigid winter air made them white, then blue, caused them to feel numb and cold and, in the end, provoked them to swell. Oh, how they stung and itched upon warming. So, protecting me today were two pairs of socks over two stockings and three layers of gloves.

Upon sneaking to the desired spot, I crouched as low as the snow allowed me and flourished the ribbons like I was waving Terra One's king's flag. Short, quick strokes of three were enough, because arousing Javala's suspicion was not my intention. I waited, listening to the wind chimes hanging off the back two corners of the house and the snap of the cloth streamers of the front two. The former were hung to ward off Vavajod's ire and the latter to appease his ego. I repeated the strokes.

The path separating the grass from the wilderness lay buried under untouched white, and a hush had fallen over the village. People were tucked away under their roofs, and here I entertained Javala's notions with trembling thighs, burning from the effort, and clacking jaws. An intense longing to warm my hands and feet by the crackle of the firewood burned through me.

I swung the handle in a long, lazy curving movement to distract myself from the comforts of the fireside. Plus, it was good to change directions to insinuate a bird's fluttering.

A gust blew in, carrying with it the bitter chill of the open fields stretching behind our residence, our home being a part of the outer boundary of our village. It knocked off my hat, rolling it along the surface of the snow toward the forest. I lunged in response. The stick flew out of my hand. I had forgotten where I was for a moment, and I ended half-buried in the snow, the chill assaulting the openings of my face.

I floundered in the soft drifts to sit, ungraceful in my movements, uttering unkind words to Vavajod, to village leaders who for years had delayed planting a tree barrier to break the westerly gusts. Without my obi belt, the slits of my longtop had ridden up to my chest along with the outer coverings and exposed what women of disrepute uncovered to the world. What a scandal and fodder for gossip it would be if someone treading the path had seen me in such a state. Shame rose to my cheeks.

I glanced at the window. There she was, standing sideways, her attention riveted on me. Crouching about, I found the ribbon tool, gave it a meek go, and then waited for Javala to become distracted. But it was like making wishes on the wind. She was a hawk, and I had to endure the snow and the chill until dark, lest she discovered me.

Half-frozen and tired, I came in through the back door, listening for noises standing apart from the usual. Except for the clatter of my teeth, silence enveloped the air. My head beat like a hammer, my fingers and toes tingled and throbbed, and despite the vigorous brushing outside the door, I shed snow on the floor.

"Did you see the bird today, Javala?" Rubbing my hands, I hurried to the hearth after changing into warmer garments.

She hovered in the same position I had seen her in from outside.

"Only some loon romping in the snow," she said, grimacing. "Unbalanced as the village drunk, that one. They didn't realize I was watching."

With another resolution in shambles, I pressed her one more time to surrender her sentiments about the cardinal, to snip the connection she had made between the comings and goings of the feathered animal and her health.

Why was I not surprised at her resistance? To believe she would yield was like asking my husband to rise from his death and rejoin our family life. Regardless, I had to persuade her to reconsider. And I was unsuccessful, as expected.

I inquired in the neighborhood for information about someone who made cardinals in wood, wool, or other forms. Good fortune shone on me when I found a woman who used her knitting needles to shape animals.

Knitted cats and snails and mice and birds and flowers overran her house's innards. While she listened to my requirement, the fine layer of dust coating them didn't escape the neat housekeeper in me. It spoke volumes about the prosperity of her business.

Realizing my need, she quoted a hefty price: two weeks' worth of pancake sales. I drove a hard bargain, as I did with my customers. She stated her reasons: the scarcity of red yarn and the difficulties of creating a bird. Her living space abounded in knitted birds—large and small, simple as well as detailed. Was she as devoid of skill and practice as she led me to believe? And judging from the crimson peeking from the heaps, she had a source for red yarn. It appeared the woman had a liking for lies and a penchant for adjusting the truth. I developed a dislike for her.

With hesitation, I assured her of my return and proceeded to the alternative: a man my neighbor had mentioned. As soon as I entered his shop, a sudden fright swarmed me, and I cried out, covering my face with my arm. All along the walls of his narrow, dingy shop were birds of prey perched on stocky branches, spying on me, their eyes full of hostility, their wings ready for a swift attack. I felt like an exposed rodent.

The owner came out chuckling from the backroom, wiping his glasses. Twitters followed him until he closed the door.

"They never fail to scare newcomers," he said. "I'm Dorsinga. Please don't fear. The birds on the walls are not alive."

"Are you sure?" I shot glances at the subjects of the conversation, my hand gripping the doorknob.

He chuckled again. "Wouldn't I know? I was the one who stuffed them."

"They are stuffed?" My hand on the door stilled.

"I swear," he said, raising his hand.

I studied him, suspicious of his manner. When he gave me ample proof for calmness, I inquired about a cardinal. Roving my eyes at the walls once more, I regarded the preserved birds with a different sentiment. They appeared full of spirit and expression despite being dead, rather impressive in their flawlessness. If I could be fooled, perhaps Javala might be too. However, she was a worldly-wise woman, unlike me. I crossed my fingers. At my silent admiration, the owner stiffened his shoulders and puffed out his chest.

"You are in luck," he said. "I have one with minor fading if you approve. I will give you a good price for it."

I abandoned the desire for a knitted bird and paid him in full. He asked for my patience since he needed a few days for preparation. The anticipation of holding a lifelike sample delighted me.

In the meantime, I devised how I intended to use the stuffed bird. Handing it to her was not worth considering. She desired him flying and twittering and foraging for food outside the window.

Two days passed, and I couldn't endure the drooping of Javala's clothes on her shrinking body anymore. I forsook our livelihood at the marketplace and collected the cardinal.

Upon arriving home, I attended to the business of the bird straight away. Self-cleansing and housework had to wait. The sooner I got Javala to believe, the more hours we would get to do what was pending.

I donned a sweater—over multiple layers—with large pockets into which I snuck a piece of string, the cardinal, and a stick foraged by the margin of the formidable place I had selected to brave. To avoid alerting Javala's sharp wits and eyesight, I took the long way through the forest to arrive at a tree in her view. The snow had melted, and the ground was soggy, but I didn't heed it. The important point was that I didn't get lost like last time. Some parts of it—although far from comfortable—were recognizable from my last ordeal.

The idea was grand and easy to implement and would take less than an hour's worth of trouble. All I had to do was scale the tree and stay hidden while dangling the cardinal for Javala, then flit it about in the branches and leaves to give an illusion of an actual bird.

It wasn't until I was behind the tree with my hands on my hips, hidden from the intended, that the hazards of the task dawned on me. The closest branch was above my head, and no amount of jumping benefited me. I don't know what overcame me that made me leap at the trunk and dig my nails in the bark. As my legs flailed and dread bloomed in my chest,

I couldn't help but think of the wall-crawling lizards—an all-absorbing subject from Javala's travels of yesteryears.

The bark came loose, and my bottom smacked the hard ground, causing a rabbit to skitter from under a bush for dear life. I nursed my rear and moaned as I searched for ways to reach my destination. Nothing inspired me except a stool. I certainly would not beg the neighbors for a ladder.

"Did a dog take a bite out of you?" Javala said as I entered, rubbing my bottom.

She never seemed to be short of things to amaze me. How alert she was to the deviations from the norm. It was this precise nature of hers that made quick closures of her spells difficult.

"Where are you carrying that off to?" she said with narrowed eyes when I swiped the stool, which, under the influence of her fantasy, had now become an extension of herself, pertinent to her role as a lookout. "You better bring that back in one piece."

"Don't you worry," I said without looking back and was out before she could string together further remarks or objections.

With the stool steadied, although inappropriate for a respectable woman, I climbed the tree and deposited myself upon a branch facing the window. Should people traversing the path glance at my confused movements above, I would not have a reputation to defend. Or rather, my reputation would balloon and precede me anywhere I dared.

As fate would have it, the stick in my pocket had snapped, and the instant I tried to remove the string—the feeble item that it was—and make do with the broken stick, the cardinal fell out of my pocket. I pounced on it with one hand. The branch I straddled was leaner and didn't appreciate my lively behavior. It cracked. The resulting jostle sent my heartbeat thrashing in my ears. I screeched. Below, people dispersed. And not long after, I came down with the tree limb like a rider landing an unruly flying horse in a whirlwind of orange and yellow leaves.

The shock tempered my wits. I grinned, lying flat on my abdomen, at the confused mass of villagers huddled beyond the expanse of the branch. Hanging jaws and widened eyes were their responses. It wasn't until I spotted some men examining the tree above that I regained my senses. I sat up and brushed myself off. My body remained covered, unlike the snow scene. Thank the Goddesses! Warmth crept to my neck and cheeks, and I wanted to disappear.

"What on earth were you doing up there?" my neighbor, who had elbowed her way through the crowd, asked. "Are you hurt? Did you break any bones?"

"Bones?" I checked my body. "I'm well."

The cardinal was not that fortunate; its headless body lay a few feet away, pieces of straw, sticks, and cotton poking out. I grabbed it and hastened to shelter, leaving the people behind to stew in their puzzlement.

"What's the rumpus about?" Javala asked.

"Nothing."

"And where is my stool?"

"I loaned it to the neighbor." I stole away to the bedchamber and slumped on a chair, wondering which body parts would be sore tomorrow.

"Nobody saw a cardinal, did they?" she said from her site.

I sighed and circled a finger across the rough outline of the bird's neck and its exposed contents.

"Javala, you *have to* eat." After three and a half days of living on water and appearing more fragile than ever, she made worry sit heavier on my shoulders, which was noteworthy because my natural disposition was cheerful. It took a lot for events or people to overwhelm and distress me.

"Eating won't make a difference."

"For sure it will. I will feed you." I rushed to serve her a meal.

She faced me. "I'm quite capable."

"Eat, then." I sat on the stool I had retrieved from the location of my last disastrous exploit. "Here's the fork."

"Your efforts are useless."

"Why would they be useless?"

"Because if the cardinal doesn't show himself by the end of the week, I'm going to die. Whether or not I gorge on food."

Oh, preserve us! I dropped the plate on the nearby table and flopped on the chair with the fork in one hand, flat-gazed, blinking slowly, for who knows how long.

A new frenzy seized me to bring Javala to her senses and keep the terrible end she forecast far off.

Now that her vigil had intensified, she abandoned her bed and prayed by the hearth. Hearing those prayers made me lose sleep at night; not because of my concern that the Goddesses or God Vavajod might fail her, but on account of the knowledge that she had been a nonreligious woman all her life. It was another sign of her spiraling descend.

My mind kept reverting to the time when her proclamations had become so dire she climbed Mount Katahorn to rescue the herbs. Apprehensive for her, my husband and I had followed. In her concern of delivering them from danger, she severed the greenery of the shrubs with a sickle, leaving behind stubbles—a state beyond any hope of regrowth. It was as bad as when she pulled the plants from the roots.

Despite six sacks full of the supposed herbal victims carried by the three of us, she continued to climb higher and higher. The terrain got rougher and the incline steeper, with the herbs fewer and farther between. Her breaths became shallower and strained. The unrestrained smile and the excited gasps she let out each time she spotted the desired vegetation when we began our task waned. Instead, she grunted with every step, pressing her hands on her thigh to bolster her leg as she ascended.

We trailed her. Unlike her, our strength was not fueled by the zeal of passion, so after a while we got tired. We begged her to submit to reality and stop. She ignored us. *How long is it going to continue?* my husband and I asked each other. We were underdressed for the descending cold of the altitude. We got our answer soon. With her strength faltering, her foot slipped, and she came tumbling toward us.

It had taken broken bones and injury to her left knee to slay her high-spirited herbal beliefs. The aftermath left her with some mental scars too. She had not stepped outside our house since then.

Just as in the previous ordeal, Javala lacked insight into her actions in the current affliction. What would her fervor steal this time? She had declared it would be her life.

I returned to the birds' preserver to find a key, a final one if available, to snap the backbone of this hardship.

"But I'm not in the business of catching birds," he said when I implored him to secure me a live specimen.

"But you must know someone who can supply one."

"Majority of my stock comes from carcass collectors. And of course, any dead birds I find on my daily walks."

"Then what is the chatter I hear in the backroom?" He had neglected to close the door to it.

"Those are my pet canaries and finches," he said with pride.

"Who brought those to you?"

"Animal trappers." He scowled, disliking the direction of the conversation.

"I just want one. Please, Jaja Dorsinga. One would be sufficient."

"It's Ja Dorsinga," he said. "I'm not married."

"Sorry, but please."

Upon noticing his reluctance, I continued, "It might help save an old woman's life." My voice broke. "A clever woman who has steered into a bit of muck."

He wrinkled his forehead and rubbed his jaw and emitted an impatient huff at my earnest appeals. I persisted. At last, he yielded. To show him my gratitude, I promised him weekend pancakes for three months along with my two weeks' income. What good was saving money if I lost Javala? Ja Dorsinga's promise came with a warning that the success depended on the animal trapper; hence, I shouldn't put too much hope and confidence in the results.

In the following days, doubts crept and took residence in my mind. A haze descended on me, making me listless and forgetful, such that managing my chores became challenging, and I became indifferent to self-care, both Javala's and mine. I jumped at every noise and tossed and turned under the blanket all night.

As the end of the week drew close, Javala became engrossed in writing instructions for me to fulfill upon her death. The only tasks I paid heed to were those of coaxing her to eat, soothing her fretting, and quieting her disturbing ideas.

Not seeing me at the market for days, my neighbor came to inquire after us. She was appalled at my state. She expressed she had never seen me unoccupied or unkempt and offered her help, but there was nothing I could assign her.

On the morning before the Javala's presumed day of death, Ja Dorsinga came calling. I fell to my knees at the threshold and squealed in such a high voice that Javala discontinued her search outdoors.

She thumped her cane against the hardened earthen floor. "Which vermin is it now?"

In Ja Dorsinga's hand swayed a metal cage. On the swing of the cage poised a little scarlet being. At first glance, I pressed my palms to my face, prayers loosening from my throat. I declared and redeclared my gratitude to the bearer and paid him in haste.

"Look, Javala, what we have here!" I held up the cage.

The black of the bird's face against the brilliance of the rest of his plumage was striking. His brisk movements were captivating. It was a quick-witted creature.

"Now, you don't have to wait by the window. You can look at him anytime your heart desires," I said, peering through the slim bars. "He is so beautiful." I wouldn't object to carving out time from my busy day to dote on him. "Who would have thought that a cardinal could match my disposition?" I had no reservations about calling the bird by his given name for the first time.

Javala's eyes gleamed with life not seen in a long time. She pulled herself up and came to the table where I set the cage. Hope for her surged within me.

Instead, she leaned on her cane and drew her gray brows in a dark scowl. "Who put him in the cage?"

"We have him now," I said with enthusiasm. "You do not need to write any of your death letters. Give up your fasting and eat heartily. I will prepare a lavish feast for us."

"He cannot be imprisoned." She raised her voice, an urgency underlining it. "Release him."

"Release him?" My grin lost its firmness. "Whatever for?"

"He is not happy. And it will not change the course of the prophecy."

"But you don't believe in the Divine Four or Their will. Not even in mad Vavajod," I said. "Why do you care about a prophecy?"

"Loose him now! Otherwise, I will not live to see tomorrow."

West gales preserve us! Her resentment was unsettling. What was I to do? The only choice was to make her see reason, so I explained and pleaded for hours, but her demand didn't bend. Exhausted, I submitted. However, I had no intention of losing the bird. The cardinal had come at a high cost, and no certainty existed in the attainment of another. I closed the front door and the one to the bedchamber. Javala stopped me as I touched my fingers to the lock of the front window.

"You misunderstand me," she said. "The bird needs to be let loose outdoors. He needs his freedom."

"If our home is suitable for us, why not for him?"

"Because he is a bird!" She slammed her fist on the table.

I recoiled. Javala considered me—her daughter-in-law—as her own and had shown the same amount of love to me as she had her single child, her son. Never in all my years living with the bright and prudent woman had she ever raised her voice or pitched her fury at me. Her compulsion had to have reached a new height.

Pressing my lips, I walked to the cage and opened its door. I crossed my arms, and glancing at her, I waited. So many painstaking plans I had undertaken and failed. What was one more?

Javala froze; the bird, not so much. Perceptive and quick, he found his freedom. He flew to the brightest spot: Javala's station—the center from where she had governed these two months, drawn by the activity that swallowed the powers of her brain, her pride, and her hunger. He crashed against the pane. I flinched and squeezed my eyes.

"There, you've done it," she said. "You know what is said about birds knocking into windows. My death is going to come—one way or another. Do as you might want, but there's no escaping it."

"The belief is about blackbirds." My chest heaved as I homed in on the bird on the floor. "Don't be birthing new notions."

The creature was confused, but alive. The collision had jarred and slowed him.

"It is equally bad for birds to fly inside a home." She extended her cane to prod him.

"No need to harass him."

She turned to the window, leaned her cane against the wall, and fussed with its lock.

"You can't let him out." I forced her hands in the opposite direction. "Why does it matter to you if he is inside or outside? Since you are so convinced that your prophecy will be fulfilled either way."

"Because a bird flying indoors could cause *your* death to come knocking on the door, too." She fought with her spare strength.

Exasperated from struggling with her, I yelled, "Good, both of us will be done with. And the cardinals of the world can go about their fanciful ways without worrying about a social call at our window."

The pitch of my voice and the bitterness in it made Javala withdraw and lean against the wall. My unfamiliar and hard-to-fathom conduct rattled me too.

The commotion spooked the bird, and he took flight. He roamed circles around the space that comprised our kitchen and living room, uttering long and sharp calls. Spellbound, we followed his movements.

"Open the door, Saati," she said as the feathery creature swooped low above her head. "This doesn't count as a sighting."

"I won't." I ducked.

"What is your intention?" She sat on her chair and got her cane ready as a weapon.

I had no plan of action; seeing the cardinal should have been reason enough for Javala's purpose to crack and crumble. She could have put the bird next to her bed to be the first vision upon awakening. There would have been no need for paper or pencils for noting its visits, no desire for sitting by the window and pouring out energy for hours. I had presumed life would retreat to its typical pattern. Or, at the very least, regular life would have been possible alongside Javala's preoccupation, except this flapping and whirling and swooping was unexpected.

She raised her cane each time the cardinal came near her, flaunting it like some great acrobat at our harvest festivals. The bird was not intimidated. He alighted on the handle of my basket, flicking its tail, moving his tiny head in short sudden starts, watching us with his beady eyes.

"Don't you dare." Javala shook the tip of her cane at the cardinal.

He stiffened the feathers on the top of his head and hopped closer. Moments later, he leaped toward her. She screamed. I winced.

The twists she performed in escaping the wrath of this creature, despite abstaining from food for days, were praiseworthy. She rolled from side to side, kicked with her sturdy leg, swung her cane around her, and folded over as though she were donning her boots. I gawked, fascinated. Next minute she twisted her arms in the air. It made me wonder if she had an undisclosed history of employment as a dagger-dodger at the carnival.

My amazement lasted while Javala engaged the bird. But when he veered and dashed at me, the wonder melted, and I dug my head into my chest and covered it with my arms. The breeze from his flutter against my skin sent a shiver through me. I shrieked. Avoiding contact with his eye, I huddled against the wall, awaiting him. Sure enough, he attacked. This time, he grazed me.

When I looked up, Javala was opening a window.

"No!" I stretched my hand in her direction.

Distracted, I didn't see the flier charge at me with its half-folded wings. Blessed Four, preserve me! I clambered onto the table, scampered backward on all limbs, and shrank in the room's corner.

The window was open, with wintry air breezing in, except the cardinal's total focus was on exacting revenge on me. I voiced more cries and dug my head in between the folds of my limbs. His persistence was undeterred. I swiped my hands in the surrounding space to strike him.

"How beautiful is he now?" Javala said in sarcasm.

"His feet are uglier than those of centipedes, and his eyes worse than a cockroach's," I said into the hollow space buried in the bundle I had formed of my body. Then the thoughts of those undesired creatures made me screech and shout.

The front door squealed. I corked my mouth and peeped from a gap in the tangle of my arms and legs, breaths shaking and heart thumping in my ears. A group of neighbors surveyed our quarters, their faces fraught with bewilderment.

Their disruption caused the cardinal to direct his energies afresh at Javala and plunge at her head. Javala—the picture of calm and strength her whole life—expressed her surprise as a howl.

Did the woman I respected and admired just howl?

The brute orbited over her and tried to land. Her wild hair, unbrushed for days, must have seemed like a bedding of gray plumage. She shooed him off. The spectacle was too dismaying for me to unglue my eyes. It was as though dreams had fashioned it.

"Stop staring at me," she said in a voice laced with panic and urgency. "Get him off me!"

I shook my head with vigor. The crawly feeling of the creatures with multiple pairs of legs, piercing mouthparts, and glassy sputtering wings hadn't left me yet. I vented a sharp cry in their memory. Then I looked at the gathering crowd in desperation, hoping to be rescued, but they had transformed into statues, bewitched by the disorder brewing in the room.

Javala swung her head, flipping her hair back and forth to discourage the bird from flittering above. Instead, they entangled his outstretched feet. He couldn't rise.

"Eek, eek!" she said.

It frightened the cardinal, and he labored to retreat but floundered, which caused her to get louder. She rose to ease the strain, but that drove him higher.

"Saaaaatiiiii," she said.

By this time, my shoulders were tight, and my palms were sweating. She had cried and begged, and someone needed to do something.

The whole time I advanced toward the stove where I kept our scissors, I wanted to flee. Images of crawlers and flapping wings coursing through me were too forceful to ignore. The door, though cramped with people, was open. I could desert the room and leave the horror behind, but I couldn't leave Javala behind.

I grabbed the scissors with clammy hands. The closer I got to her, the worse I trembled. This was how she must feel day after day with her constant shaking. I remembered my promise to my husband, and it gave me strength, making my steps more assured.

I grabbed her upper arm and demanded her to hold still. As soon as she did, I cut the strands that bound the bird to her. Unleashed, the bird scrambled to the open window and out.

Exhausted from the toil and burned from the surge of emotions, Javala collapsed to the floor. The villagers rushed in to carry her to the bed.

Once the neighbors were gone, I lay beside her, my spent body in want of repose but my mind too spirited to doze. So, I brushed her hair. After a while, I rubbed and kneaded her legs, as I often did to improve their strength, until night fell. Thereupon, I lit a lamp and read to her one of her books.

The next morning Javala's side of the bed was empty but made. Fearing a disastrous situation, I ran out to the living room. The sight startled me. She was dressed and groomed and was fanning the kindling to build a flame in the stove, like on occasions in the old days, when I had sickened and couldn't awaken on time. The dead silence of profound awe gripped me.

"The market doesn't wait for loiterers," she said.

When I didn't stir, she took out the bowls and the flour and got to cracking the eggs. It was the knock of the fourth egg against the wooden counter that dulled my shock and jerked me back to reality. I greeted her.

"Why don't you rest? I'll get your meal." I guided her frail body over to the table, grateful that her fall had shattered no bones or torn her skin.

As I turned, my eyebrows shot up on noticing the change in the furniture. The chair and the stool, which had stood as sentry by the window for so long, were gone.

"I've already had an early breakfast. I was famished," she said. "I can chop some herbs while sitting here."

Handing her a knife and parsley, I busied myself at the stove and placed a pan on the heat. The bird was gone, but the sear of the encounter was still raw. Yet the itch to know the fate of Javala's preoccupation was undeniable.

"Are you going to watch for the cardinal today?" I said, despite the risk of dire consequences. Although I made it sound as gentle as I could.

"What cardinal?" Javala said.

I lifted my face to the wall before me.

What about herbs? she had said at the termination of her herb compulsion. So, was this new question of hers a spark in the darkness?

"The bird whose sighting you pined for every day," I said.

"Why would I get involved in such a useless activity?"

She lacked memories of the feathered animal, just as she had about the so-called witch's curse at the end of the herbal experience. I smiled. The original Javala had prevailed. And unlike the herb situation—thank the gales—she had gotten away with a few bruises and some shortened strands of tangled hair.

I removed Ja Dorsinga's headless fake from my pocket, studied it with silent relief, and added it to the collection on the shelf when I was satisfied.

4

— · —

COLLECTIBLES

D jinn kept himself inconspicuous most days. Today, though, was
different. As I snuck out of Bergamot's fenced-in compound and
got comfortable in my gait along the dirt path bordered with wide blades
of grass, he cleared his throat.

I closed my eyes and sighed.

The goats were in the enclosed pasture now, udders empty from milk-
ing. Washed clothes hung on the line, limp from want of moving air,
and the scrubbed utensils from breakfast lay draining on the towels. The
house was spotless, at least as clean as I could make it, considering its age
and the bare, dry soil everywhere outdoors. And the pigs . . . brutes! They
had barged in, trampling my feet, sniffing and snickering, warring to get
their snouts in the trough even before I had tipped in the first bucket of
feed. At a glance, one would think they had heard a battle call. I fled their
murderous frenzy, only to plummet into a watering trough. Savages!

Anyway, through those hours, huddled in some corner or other, Djinn
was present. He was always present, whether or not I perceived him,
watching me go through the motions of the day. Today, however, he
assumed a physical form, as real as a rock or the horse or the furniture.
And now he was on my tail.

A groan rose from within me. One hour was what I had before the
overhead sun inched its way toward the horizon, before my remaining
responsibilities pressed their weight again on me.

He attempted to snag me into a conversation, not outright with words, but with frequent voluntary hiccups, cracking and popping of joints, lip-smacking, and other such bodily noises. It took sheer force of will to keep me insulated from it. I managed it well until he belched, after which my entire focus surrendered to guessing his subsequent action and the anticipation of its arrival. When he began his whistling and whooshing, my tolerance disintegrated.

"Why are you following me?" I said with a hint of sharpness, speeding my steps, depriving him of the pleasure of a glance.

"I'm not, Naaz," he said in a throaty voice. "This path is the lone way to get to where the air is purest."

"But a djinn can go anywhere, can't he?"

He went silent, and the insects resumed their trilling. I imagined them shaking off their fear and emerging from spots they had ducked into at the abrupt and foreign sounds emanating from two graceless beings. The dry season was long and filled with scorching afternoons on Najik, an island situated close to Terra Six as informed by my follower. What dew struggled to form in the temperate hours of the morning disappeared before its process was completed. For most of the year this was so, except for a window of three months when full-bellied, crackling clouds darkened the sky and brought relief. I tolerated the swelter and the parched earth as long as I wasn't asked to labor outdoors under the fury of the punishing sun.

Part of the underbrush, wild carrot flower heads caught by the breeze swayed in agreement, their carroty fragrance permeating the space. I plucked one and tucked it in the belt of my dress; the flower head stood out as a jewel against the gray cloth, its flat-topped, lacey structure vivid in contrast to my brown skin. Ahead, tiny star-shaped blossoms drew my attention next. Then in view were the tall spears, white-hot like metal rods sitting in fierce fire for too long, except their forms were soft and spicy-smelling and startled birds bolted from them at the sound of my step.

I forgot about my follower until I was halfway up to the patch of earth where trees stood in clumps, framing majestic views and funneling a pathway for the most delicious winds. When I looked back, I couldn't see him past the curves, so I waited, unsure why. His habit of being around me since childhood, I guessed.

He finally walked around the bend, dressed unlike any of the men who visited my adopted father, Bergamot. The looseness of his full-sleeved shirt, pleats at the collarbones, and the shirt's untucked state made him appear larger than usual. The gold of his embossed pendant, resting at the base of his neck, flashed as it caught the sun. His hair, milky-white, the top of which was pulled back and tied, was loose around his neck. I blinked. With the way the rays fell around him, he looked like a celestial being. The beginnings of a smirk emerged on his face upon seeing me. I whirled, warmth rising to my cheeks, and strode onward.

Djinn could be soundless if he wanted, similar to Bergamot's black cats, but after about half a mile I couldn't resist, and I peeked over my shoulder. His closeness startled me.

"You will get in trouble if he knows you break the rules," he said.

"I know Bergamot orders you to watch my doings," I continued, my back to him. "You've been at it since I was a baby."

"Supervise is the right word," he said, increasing the pitch of his voice. "You are a child."

"Child?" I rolled my eyes. "I'm sixteen! And I follow every rule except the one about leaving the enclosure. And I always come back. So, he shouldn't have a problem with me."

"And he doesn't because he doesn't know. I haven't told him." He changed the sound of his voice again.

"So then why are you following me? I know you don't blindly pursue your master's word. You're good at steering Bergamot's demand in a way that suits your desire. And yet he cannot say you violated his command. So don't tell me you're doing your duty."

"I'm shadowing you because I enjoy your company."

I snorted.

"You are hundreds of years old, millions even. Why do you want to befriend a *child*?"

"I thought you said you were not a child," he said, changing his tone.

Today he played with his voice, displayed the spectrum much the same as a rainbow. Sometimes it was his attire; other times, it was the denseness of his body.

On and on, we strolled in silence, Djinn dawdling behind me. So much in my life was directed by my adoptive father. This walk of long strides, however, granted me a morsel of power and independence, the ability to direct my hour in the way I desired, without scrutiny or judgment. I gulped in the refreshing air. The blue of the sky was breathtaking, almost miraculous. My eyes, no matter where they roamed, settled back on the depth and vastness of it, as if it was a code my mind couldn't decipher, as if the memory of its existence was short lived. Its striking color compelled me to return to it again and again to refresh my understanding of its beauty.

The air was sweeter and lighter here than in the compound below. Papery seeds, carried by its feathery inverted umbrellas four times its size, drifted past me. Where were they heading? What destiny awaited them? Oblivious, they seemed cheerful in the moment, happy to be moving, confident they would be whisked to a welcoming place to root.

"Do you know where Bergamot keeps me?" Djinn said after a while, startling me out of my reverie. "My vessel, I mean."

My brows knitted. "Why would I know? Why would I want to know when you are always around me as a sentry?"

He didn't bother me for a few yards, then, "Do you know Bergamot's a collector?"

Why was Djinn bringing these subjects up? He wasn't revealing any-thing unfamiliar. Was he so spiritless?

"You mean he hoards things," I said, placing one foot in front of the other. Every building except for the food storehouse and the living spaces for us and the animals were crammed with items. Bergamot had never enlightened me on their purpose, and I never inquired. Because when I had, he had gotten spiteful and declared it was no concern of mine. And from then on, I kept it so.

"Do you approve of the strangers coming and going at odd hours?" he said.

"The old man is trying to make a living for him and me. Why is it wrong?" I wiped my forehead with the cotton towel hanging limp at my right hip, one corner knotted at the belt and the other grazing halfway down the skirt of my long dress. "Besides, my approval has no clout."

"Some living indeed!" He sounded loud and severe.

I frowned and turned. My overseer had made comments of resentment about his master on a few occasions, and again I felt caught in between. "What do you mean?"

"Why do you alternate between the three unvarying dresses? Wear one while the other two dry on the line? When did you eat anything besides the standard staples he provides for you to cook and serve? Did he ever splurge on an item of entertainment for you? Where does the money from his sales go? And the most important of all—why does he imprison you in the compound?"

If he went that route, I had to defend Bergamot. Although he never behaved as a father should and often intimidated me with his sharp words and severe eyes, Bergamot never beat me. He didn't bother me if I followed his rules and averted his hunger with meals served on time.

"I've got a roof over my head, a bed to sleep in, and food in my belly. What else do I need?" I turned to glare at him, a flush of heat rising to my face. "I was a toddler bawling and covered in dust while every villager lay dead. Pierced by either a sword or an arrow. My hamlet pillaged and burned by raiders. Bergamot found me, and I'm grateful for his generosity."

Djinn chuckled.

I glowered at him.

"Ever wondered why you were the sole survivor?" His voice was steady this time.

I folded my hands against my waist. "Because my mother hid me well. It was the crying that caught Bergamot's attention."

He cocked his head toward the side of his facial scar. "And he happened to be . . . just passing by?"

The material of my dress clung to me, restrictive, the belt too tight. I tugged at the belt's knot. The flower slipped to my feet, and I crushed it under my shoe. Djinn was doing such a fantastic job at his conversation—he had wound me in it like the string around a spinning-top toy.

"I get about an hour to myself. So, say what you want to say, and leave me alone."

"Okay," he said. "You—like the piles of antique furniture and the mountains of books, the rugs, silver and earthenware, and the wall art, all the goods crammed in the various buildings—are nothing more than a collectible. A highly prized one. Like me."

My jaw fell open. Me, a collectible—what ridiculous nonsense.

I glanced at the expanse of the flat land at the top of the hill, a short distance away. The grass there was as green as the algae coating the water-filled ditches on either side of the fallen tree I used, as a bridge, to sneak out of Bergamot's enclosure. Djinn had wasted so much of my time in a foolish exchange.

"I think you should return to your urn and stay there until I come back. You can continue your vigil after I've had some carefree time. Alone."

His features brightened. "How did you know I was in an urn?" Delight oozed through his wide-open eyes. "You *do* know about its location."

If he could grab my arm, he would have, and I was grateful djinns couldn't grasp things.

Surprised, I shouted at him. "No, I don't!" I was perturbed at how he had latched on to the idea. "Leave me."

I discovered him floating behind me the following day. "Back at it again?" I said.

"My master gave me one assignment, and you are it."

I rolled a lazy glance over him. A patchwork of light filtering through the Mimo tree covered his body. My eye swept up the branch overhanging the path and lingered on the clusters of pink flowers. They were my favorite. Often, I snuck out of the compound with needle and thread. Then, sprawled on the cool grass on the hill, I wove a garland out of a towelful of those flowers, the delight of which was only curtailed by time constraints. It hung around my neck, its silky parts tickling me, pleasing me, perfuming me until I reached the fence. There, I discarded them. The pink circles floating on the mossy-colored surface of the ditches made such a pretty sight.

"You can stay here until the end of the hour," I said. We were a quarter of the way out. "I promise you of my return."

"That is the problem," he said with no shifts in voice or looks or other such things. As he had mentioned long ago, his fluctuating behavior ensued when boredom braced him, and life seemed bland and redundant to the point of hopelessness. Imagine a life of captivity. Especially when it extended for years and years and years, with no end in sight. Who wouldn't be wearied?

"Why is the assurance of my return a problem?" I said.

He appeared hesitant. It was peculiar. In my life span of knowing him, he was everything except reluctant, indecisive, or fearful.

"Timidity doesn't suit you," I said.

He rubbed his dimpled chin, his stare heavy with a burden I wasn't sure I wanted to shoulder.

I half-turned to continue to my special place when he said, "Have you ever thought of escaping?"

His question jarred me, making me stall. "Escaping? To where?" I faced him, baffled. "And why?" With puffs of pink, the Mimo branches above and behind him rose and fell in response to the breeze's push. "I'm content here." I rubbed the back of my neck. "Why are you doing this? Aren't you supposed to be Bergamot's eyes and ears? Shouldn't you be complying with his wish?"

"Did you think about what I revealed yesterday?" he said.

"About me being a collectible?" I raised my eyebrows. "The silliest notion I ever heard. How can a person be a collectible?"

The heaviness in his gaze was replaced by amusement, as if he was privy to a secret. "They are if they are priceless."

"Washing and cleaning and cooking kind of value?"

"Such duties anyone can fulfill. No, I mean—one of a kind, invaluable."

I chuckled.

"The kind he hires raiders to ensure the acquisition of," he continued.

I swallowed, my saliva ropy. The moment stretched on, and the gravity of the accusation pressed on me, challenging me to dig deeper, however incorrect it felt.

"Are you—are you saying he caused the bloodbath at my hamlet? The—the death of my parents, my grandparents? Merely to get *me*?" I waited for an answer, but none came. "Very well, why am I special?"

"You can start a fire," he said, unblinking.

A bark of a laugh burst out. *Start a fire.* If I kept a count of how many times I did *that* during the day . . . I let his words land, and the longer they roosted, the more absurd the idea became. It made me think of the silly game of pursuing a runaway chicken: its feet pattering against the ground as it half-ran, half-flew away from the coop, dashing left and right, slipping under inconceivable hiding spaces, clucking in mockery at my clumsiness. The more I considered his presumption, the more nonsensical it felt until I pitched over before him, drowning in laughter, my cheeks and sides aching. Then, when I could get a breath in, I said, "If nothing else, I can depend on you for amusement."

He wasn't amused.

"You are thinking too small," he said, leaning against a tree. "I don't mean using flint to light the firewood in the hearth, or to spark a candle or lantern's flame or in the stove to cook a meal. Nor igniting par-par blocks for light or energy. Nor a bonfire to burn the brush. Of course, you could do those if you wished. But I'm talking about blazes. I'm speaking of you sparking a sea of flames enough to burn a person, a house, a village, a forest. Curtains of fire. Showers. Flares shooting out of your pointer fingers. And the ability to curb it, too, with the turn of your wrist and closure of your fist."

I found the description so outrageous, my mind went blank, and I gawked at him in dumb stupor.

"You think Bergamot cares about the possessions he shoves in his buildings?" Djinn said. "He stopped amassing items after he found you."

"How can I believe you?" I said. "People magic receded after the holy Sigils disappeared from our world four hundred and fifty years ago. Only certain items blessed by or connected to the Sigils in some form retained it. You were the one who told me about it. Even you're affected, your powers and abilities. And you're saying I've had this magic for sixteen years?"

"I don't know how it's possible. For all we know, it could be feeble, diluted. Doesn't matter because having this power is significant," he said. "Bergamot's biding his time, waiting for the right buyer. You are his ultimate passage to renown and wealth. When he finds a suitable patron, he'll scurry out of the hovel he calls home to be cradled into a household of luxury, in a city somewhere. Perhaps he wishes to sell you to the king of Terra Two, who has aims of becoming an emperor."

His ideas were insane. If I were to question the motives of a person, it would be him, not Bergamot. The men coming and going were buyers, yes, but they also came to sell their wares, physical items. I had seen them, both the items and the men. They snuck no furtive glances. They didn't pause their conversations when I appeared to serve them water or other refreshments. It was what men of business did. However, to pin selfish motives on a man who . . . Djinn had even muddled my conviction that Bergamot was my savior. And what was this madness about my ability to spur a storm of fire upon our world of seven continents and numerous islands, our Sigilis Septerra?

"Are you testing my loyalty?" My temperature rose. "Who sells human beings in these times anyway?"

"You are distrustful of me and doubting what I shared?" he questioned me from under his dark brows. "You have a terrible future ahead of you. One of abuse and captivity. Smokes, you've been imprisoned for years and you can't even recognize it."

"Well, maybe no buyer will come forth." I tracked the sun.

"Do you want to chance your life against it? Because the old man doesn't. He goes to the market every week seeking buyers, putting the word out to the vilest crud out there!" His arm lashed out in the air in exasperation.

He was taking this too seriously, and exhaustion was creeping along my legs.

"How do you know this?" I said.

"I'm a djinn!"

"One whose abilities have seen better days."

He pressed his lips together.

"Why are you telling me this?" I said.

"Because I want you to act." Fervor filled his voice.

"If you are suggesting killing Bergamot, I won't do it. I can't even hurt an ant."

He shook his head.

"Then what?"

"I suggested it already." He descended the path, leaving me scowling.

I plopped my bottom on a rock midway to my destination and remained for the spare time, studying the insect life instead of being cushioned by the softness lining the base of the oaks and observing the varying hues of the valley and the sea below.

Later at night, my sleep was interrupted by ifs and buts and what-ifs and a multitude of scenarios associated with them. These carried into the following day's hours and affected my concentration on my daily chores.

"I tried lighting the kindling with my pointer," I said when Djinn harrumphed a few steps behind me the next day to announce his presence. "Nothing happened."

A conversation with him never started on my end, but this time it did, and I assumed it was because of my eagerness to disprove his charges.

"Did you walk the minute you were born?" he said. "Or learn to speak without being read and talked to?"

In my need and eagerness to rebuff him, this detail had evaded reflection. "So, I need lessons? From whom?"

"Is that your priority?"

Once again, we sheltered in the shade of the Mimo tree. He was in his full-body form in a shirt as bright as his teeth.

"You want me to run away?"

A shine flooded the darkness of his eyes. Why did I sense he had concocted a plan and manipulated the circumstances, and I was the midpoint of a storm?

"If you dare to implicate me, or if the old man gets suspicious because of your lack of discretion . . . I will deny and condemn the plot," he said.

Breathe of a conspiracy in Bergamot's ear? Me? I had no influence on him. My words held no weight, and I had never been able to sway his decisions on any subject. On the contrary, my eyelids twitched, and my shoulders tightened every time I had to explain myself to him. In those moments, I became self-conscious of how he viewed my smile, my words, and the faulty conclusions he drew, making me doubt my own character and reality.

"But you are telling the truth about the talent," I said, surprising myself. Why was I indulging Djinn? My routine and responsibilities were clear and satisfactory to both Bergamot and me.

"I swear on my urn."

After a while, under the oaks, I gave the fresh revelations a thorough examination, and no matter how hard I strived to believe Djinn, the doubts were unavoidable. I couldn't halt the burgeoning natural curiosity regarding his motives, his aspirations. Ignoring them was impossible, particularly when he had steered me in this direction, even though there was a possibility of what pigs made with mud and water—a muck, except bigger. What future lay waiting for me, or rather, what tragedies? One blunder would lead to another.

And what of my temptations?

Recklessness, it was utter recklessness.

T he succeeding day, once again, I had company as I broke away from the compound to get to my favorite spot.

"How is your mind?" Djinn asked, his bottom half a mass of trailing smoke, curling and swirling, as alive as his features.

"Is that your way of asking if I have made any plans?"

He cradled a branch of borberry bush and studied the bell-shaped flowers, lavender and the size of my thumbnail. Since he rippled the water, he'd distanced himself, pretending the idea originated from me and he had no part in it. But I knew his quirks and habits and the nature of his being. He had been my guardian and teacher since my ayah had been sent packing at age six, even if it was directed by Bergamot.

"I need proof," I said. "Any."

"It is impossible." He brushed the palm of his other hand along the bountiful branch. Of course, neither hand touched the bush; they were disembodied, same as the rest of him.

"I thought you were a djinn."

"But I'm supposed to oversee you and your activities."

"Who's to know if you disappear somewhere while I'm on the hill for an hour? I don't tattle."

He opened and closed his mouth, fiddled with the ornaments around his wrists, round polished stones of yellow. Was it possible he was as uncomfortable about this affair as me?

"You cannot retract now. Considering you've told me I'm capable of magic."

Moments passed.

Before retreating, Djinn said one word: "Tomorrow."

N ext day, as I replaced the tall piece of the fence after leaving the compound and tottered across the fallen tree, Djinn flew past and startled me. If I plunged toward the hidden dangers of the ditch underneath, he would be useless. By the time he scurried and brought Bergamot to my rescue, my secret would be exposed, or I would be dead.

Once on stable ground, I was about to admonish him when he said, "I'm leaving."

"Finally, an hour without an overseer," I said. "Oh, what joy and peace."

"Souse your excitement." His face was as though he had been force-fed spoiled meat. "I'll go each day during your respite time. Until I find your proof."

He left, and my hour was awash with lazy wonder.

I didn't see Djinn until I returned. He was sulking in the kitchen, quiet as he was every day. No proof was good news.

Over the years, he had been warned repeatedly by Bergamot against befriending me, and today, as usual, he upheld his master's expectation. No words were exchanged between us, and I ignored him. Chores needed my attention.

Over the next four days, my breaks were spent in the company of nature alone, and I was grateful to forget the distress and uneasiness Djinn had aroused.

"You're back," I said when he hovered close to me. My neck rested on the rolled towel, and my attention was snatched by wispy clouds sailing past a patch of striking blue.

He deposited himself beside me. Not in the genuine sense of the word, but the best he could do with his gauzy form.

"You don't look too happy," he said.

He had always been a perceptive observer.

"You will resume your charge," I said. "One tires of being constantly spied on."

He craned his neck upward, the clouds as ethereal as him.

"Well, did you accomplish anything?" I said.

"When you go home, put your pointer in the fire," he said. "Just the pointer."

I cocked my head at him.

"That is all." He stood and glided away.

Did he think this was a game? I was not interested in burning my body part and gifting myself a permanent disfigurement in a quest to quell my curiosity. What was in it for him anyway? Why did he prod me so?

As usual, I carried on with my housework for the rest of the day, but the foolishness Djinn had implanted nagged at me. So finally, after I removed the pot of rice from the fire, I gave my finger a quick sweep through the flames. Of course, I had to go slow. Therefore, I did. The rest of the hand sensed the heat, but not the pointer. I clamped my jaw and made a third pass, slower still. I got the same result.

Glancing about and finding no one around, not even Djinn, I sucked in a breath and advanced the tip toward the center, then held it in the fire for a count of ten. A faint odor of singed skin arose, but no pain erupted. I continued holding my finger there, waiting for the agony to flare, but except for the skin reddening, reminiscent of fresh meat . . . nothing. Upon withdrawal, the skin held its unnatural color for a few minutes, then was restored to its original shade.

I was shaken to my core; I forgot my duties and ran to my bed and collapsed, tears wetting my face, wishing for a reversal to the state of ignorance.

"You need to hasten." Djinn was in my room.

I jumped out of my bed, confounded, my face wet.

"You are not allowed in my room." I glanced at the open door, afraid of Bergamot's wrath streaking in like unannounced lightning.

"I'm sorry," Djinn said.

"Are you?" My eyes flitted to the shadows at the door frame. The urge to air my displeasure as him having crossed a boundary, sprouted. "I've never known you to have remorse."

"After I left you today, I loitered in our town's square and a few others, eavesdropping for information. The old man has found you a buyer. He is to arrive tomorrow."

When I didn't react, he said, "Do you understand? He is due tomorrow."

My mind was too dulled by the shock of discovery to process his request and launch into a flurry of activity for my future. I sat at the side of my bed, forgetting the rice and Bergamot, clutching my pillow to my chest, glancing at the surrounding objects and seeing nothing.

"You cannot afford to waste time."

I glanced at him with the same dead glance I gave the items in my room.

I awoke with a start when I heard Bergamot call me from the threshold. The fool had gone and gotten the old man when his prodding hadn't fruited.

"What is the matter with you?" Bergamot said. "Your tasks are unfinished. How can you idle at this hour when I deny my old bones the rest for which they so often beg? Get up! I'm hungry."

I sprang and ran out of my room with an apology. The kitchen continued to roast. Heat entering the southern windows augmented the abundance generated from cooking. I found Djinn lurking in the corner.

"I don't appreciate you making trouble for me," I whispered with hostility.

"You call this trouble?" he whispered back. "You should be afraid of what's coming."

No sooner had he finished than Bergamot stepped into the kitchen.

"I want an account on her before bed," he said to Djinn with his stern voice and piercing eyes. "And no discourse with her of any kind. I don't need major provocation to permanently lid your urn."

With my head hanging, I pulled out a plate and plonked two scoops of ghee-browned stinging nettles and okra on it.

"You see how he relishes threatening people?" Djinn said when Bergamot left. "You need to pack essentials in between your responsibilities. And don't forget the food."

Everything was so rushed. Until now, I had been convinced Djinn's suggestions were his opinions and not the truth, and I had been focused on a game of ridding myself of him for an hour of dreamy sluggishness. But since the experiment with the fire, I'd felt caught in a swarm of starving, aggressive pigs, being jostled and tackling exasperation.

I heaped rice next to the vegetables.

Was Djinn to be trusted about the story of the buyer? He had been truthful about my unnatural ability. And did I have the courage to desert the life, the comfort, I'd known? (I remembered nothing of my former life.) Throw it away? But if Djinn's concern was genuine and I didn't take action, then what? My life would transform either way. Although it was wiser to be in control of it than not.

I moved the ladle over the rice, pouring the bean stew in circles, then repeated it two more times.

The thoughts of the escape and the actions I needed to take—the details—before I headed to the loosened piece of the fence were soberly unexplored until now. And what of the route?

"Bergamot padlocks the gate of the compound," I said. "And the depths of the ditch at the fence are unknown. It's filled with murky water and surrounded by cragginess. Remember, I don't swim. Also, the path is bordered by dense, disorienting woods. And the drop on the other side of the hill is steep and littered with jagged, uneven rocks. How do you want me to escape?"

This was half-baked, and it made me want to bite my nails—a habit forced out by Bergamot's ruler on my fingers.

"I'll guide you." A smile bloomed on his face.

"You know the way?" Of course he did; he was a djinn. But when he twisted his hands together and gave me a downcast expression, I said, "Why are you hesitating?"

"There's one more thing."

I signaled for him to go on.

"Do you know where the old man keeps me? My vessel?"

"Why question me about it again?" I narrowed my eyes at him.

"Do you know?"

"No."

He let out a long sigh and pinched the bridge of his nose.

Suddenly, the pieces fell into place. I abandoned the plate on the table.

"You began this whole situation because *you* wanted *your* freedom," I said, to which he looked away. "You had no actual concern for me. I am a means to further your cause. Isn't it so?"

He couldn't meet my eye.

"Tell me I'm wrong. Tell me!" I wished he could taste the bitter tang in my mouth and feel the burn surging in my throat. "A girl of sixteen who's prepared to leave her universe behind and enter the frightening unknown, and you can't even give her your reason?"

I wanted to fling the scalding rice in his face, but it wouldn't hurt him. I wanted to scream and curse him, but Bergamot was somewhere close.

The confidence he carried around his jaw and shoulder and in his eyes was gone.

"We are both counting time till the old man sells us," he said. "I'd rather be with a master identical to you than another man resembling him. In your freedom, I saw mine. Is that so bad?"

My eyes fixed on him, hard and intense. Forgiveness was unthinkable in that moment, and the tightness of my lips and jaw made it known to him.

"Describe your urn."

He shrugged.

"How can you not know? You've lived in it for centuries."

"I'm familiar with the inside. Clay. But the outside . . . I'm cursed to be forever blind to its location and forgetful of its appearance. To prevent me from attempts at devising, colluding, and acting on a wicked plan."

"That is, until you find an idiot, witless enough to conspire with you."

"That's not how I would describe you. Discard what Bergamot has hammered into you, day after day, through the totality of your life here. It's another reason for you to flee."

I peered at the space beyond the kitchen door. Late-afternoon light poured in through its open windows, and in them I saw motes of suspended dust. Options opened for me: I could stay enclosed within the walls, among the dust and the trapped heat. Or I could choose to be free. Rise above to breathe unfettered air. It would be akin to a perennial existence in my favorite area on the hill.

When I returned to Djinn's face with my temper allayed, he said, "If it helps, I was told my urn's simple."

"It's not useful. Clay urns are common, and they are all simple."

Ambiguity made me uncomfortable, and I surveyed the shelf of urns and pitchers and bottles until I could express it.

"Running away with your stolen urn will make me your master? I thought djinns and their vessels were bound by rules," I said.

"If you could live for a day inside the vessel," he said, "you'd be so soaked in the rules you would never want to mention them, ever. They are scribbled on every space available. The rules will stare at you every waking moment and even make their impression behind closed eyelids when you sleep. They are unfading, indestructible. When imprisoned with them for decades at a time, the rules can stifle your thoughts, your breath, your life. Madness would be a relief. But if you want to know—"

"A few basic ones." I couldn't proceed without understanding.

His shoulders and facial features sagged.

"One," he said. "If the urn is stolen, the thief becomes my new master . . . upon my approval. Otherwise, I won't let it end well with the robber. Two, if both my master and I desire to forfeit the partnership and a new owner agrees to possess the urn, he becomes my master. Of course, both my current master and I are required to permit the change. This has never happened to me." He got closer. "Regardless of the rules, someone has to be the owner of the urn the entire time, and my master has more power over me than vice versa."

"How long does it take you to get me my supper?" Bergamot's annoyance carried forth from the veranda. "I'll make you reheat it if it is cold."

The old man preferred steaming food in searing weather. It was a wonder the routine hadn't yet melted off his tongue and he hadn't swallowed it by mistake.

"What if the owner dies?" I said.

"Then the discoverer becomes the new master irrelevant to my liking. Until then, I either suffocate inside if the vessel is closed or can powerlessly roam free if not. Having a master influences my abilities."

"And when the urn cracks or breaks?"

"I die."

"Naaz!" Bergamot said. "Are you deaf?"

I rushed to serve another plate.

"I'll meet you on the porch of the red cabin. But first, my chores." I hurried to the veranda with the meal, steam rising to my sweaty face.

After Bergamot's snores reached my room, I hoisted the sack over my shoulder and snuck out. I had amassed essentials between the time my responsibilities ended and when the creaking of Bergamot's bed ceased.

The sack contained clothing, notepaper, an ink pen with a full cartridge, a knife, two candles, a box of matchsticks, and the lightest pan the kitchen offered. Edibles included dried berries, onions, flatbread, dry corn and beans, uncooked sorghum, and salt. And of course, water.

The water container was Bergamot's favorite, a sturdy bottle constructed of metal with a leak-free plug. He carried it everywhere: to the market, to the field where a few laborers helped him with crops, to his seat on the veranda, and to his bed. It freed him from worrying about water or staying close to the kitchen, near the water pot, to quench the constant thirst the weather imposed on us. Despite his efforts, he hadn't found another. I couldn't wager on which would make him angrier, losing his container or the desertion by his most valuable collectible.

The sky was bejeweled with stars, and the moon was two or three days shy of its full glory. Fortunately, the curtains of Bergamot's front-facing room were drawn. The night air was still and dusty, and the heat of the day radiated from the ground. There was no trace of the three buckets of water I had doused the dirt and the veranda with earlier, my nightly routine to keep the grit suppressed and the ground cool.

The red cabin was near the loose board of the fence. Djinn pointed to the key hidden in the rafter when I stepped on the porch. With the sack secure behind the shelter, I entered and lit a candle. Disturbed dust ushered in with each breath made me cough, and Djinn looked at me in alarm. Layers of it coated every surface. I tsked, grateful Bergamot hadn't added the daunting task of cleaning these storage areas to my existing list, already long to begin with. I continued the search, covering the lower half of my face with the towel hanging from my belt.

Empty-handed, we advanced to the adjoining cottage. Then to the one beside the padlocked gates, at the opposite end. And then to its adjacent structure.

We were running out of buildings, and hours were rolling away. I doubted our search. Had we missed it? We were . . . rather, I was crusted in a membrane of sweat and dust. We should have planned this better, should have spent a few days or nights in the search first, separate from the escape night.

I plopped on the wooden floor in between two chairs, my face buried in my hands. Uncertainty thrust its way through. The hope of liberation—which had required so much of persuasion to germinate—evaporated in the night air. And with its parting, fear entered.

"Naaz," Djinn whispered.

"What if it is in his room? By his bed?" I said, not looking up.

"It isn't. Bergamot boasted about it once."

I glanced at Djinn. My optimism had burned down with the candle as the night progressed. If this venture failed, tomorrow would be a slog. A night vigil was never good.

"He bragged it was 'so well hidden among his collectibles, no one could find it,'" Djinn said. "Hidden in plain sight, same as us, I guess."

It got me thinking.

"So why are we searching among the furniture and rugs?" I said. "We should look among brown knickknacks."

"The shed," we said together.

On silent feet and with Djinn beside me, I raced to the shed. A creak from the door pierced the quiet of the night.

"Careful," Djinn said as soon as I lifted my foot to take my first step inside.

Wooden planks angled from the top left to the center of the floor. Without his warning, I would have tripped and caused them to slide and smash the other objects in the overcrowded interior, not to mention my potential injuries. The racket would be loud enough to awaken the property owner and end our adventures.

With the candleholder secure on the crowded top of a short bookshelf, I studied the place. I sighed. So many articles hoarded. In the areas where the light reached, layers upon layers of unorganized antique books, drab yarn, furry coats, jars, crockery, musical instruments, ornate wooden boxes, and more stood smothered in dust. Perilous towers of uneven objects threatened to teeter at a touch, one step away from shattering its own items and wrecking the surrounding ones.

Last I had been here was years ago. When had it gotten so bad? Or was it because I had been too young to perceive what it truly was? Were these items truly valuable, fetching a steady income, and not rubbish? Or was it Bergamot's veil to prevent me from discovering his secret? Whatever it was, I didn't have the energy to sift through the disorder.

"Can you spot any urns?" I asked my partner.

"The old man is twice as wide as you and clumsy," he said.

I frowned.

"He cannot go pattering through this jumble," he said. "So, either there is a hidden path, or the urn is somewhere closer to the entrance."

"Why would he want easy access to the urn?"

"Because he is forever threatening to shut its lid. He knows I fear confinement."

Djinn could roam around in the shed without trouble, but his eyesight wasn't better than mine. So even if he floated in the farthest corners, the shadows wouldn't reveal their mysteries. And the candle didn't offer the best light, but by pointing it in each direction, we agreed on the absence of an obvious pathway broad enough to accommodate a person.

I searched closer. The short bookcase adjoining the entrance sat at an angle.

"Bookcases are usually thrust against a wall," Djinn said.

As soon as I furthered the candle behind it, a glint flashed.

At a glance, I could tell the urn was special. The interior, devoid of any marks, was made of clay as Djinn had remarked, but the mantle was where he was wrong. Its material was one I'd never encountered: smooth and light and burlap brown. Then there was its atypical shape. The urn had two parts of equal size. The base was in the shape of a cup, and the lid, tapering in pudgy layers, ended in an inverted teardrop. At the outside edges of both halves, ancient marks were chiseled and filled with gold, and the rest of the outer surface was covered in a script of illegible language. Was it a spell? A curse? A mystical saying or a poem?

"This is nowhere near ordinary," I said, displaying the gold to Djinn.

I brought the lid closer to the base, thinking how the two would fasten with a defined lip across the middle. Djinn cried out. His eyes were wide, the whites showing.

Upon realizing my error, I dropped my hands to my sides and said, "I won't close it."

"We have to hurry," he said upon overcoming his shock. "Elopement is best under a cape of darkness."

I extinguished the candle, shut the door, and stood before it until its creak dissipated in the night's quiet. Then I scampered across the compound, mindful of the curtain blanketing Bergamot's window, and of the cats roaming the area, as dark as the surroundings and the night sky.

As soon as I reached behind the red cabin, I submitted the urn parts to my sack, careful to keep them apart. We left through my secret exit and climbed the hill under the light of the swollen moon. A strong gale rustled the forest trees on the right of the path as if trying to awaken them and stop the escapees. Halfway up, Djinn led me into the darkness of the woods.

The only time he spoke was to warn me: "Be careful. Don't drop the urn."

His dwelling was going nowhere. It jangled with the inkwell, the knife, and the pan in the sack whose knot had settled into the groove of my right shoulder and whose bulk poked my back. But I dared not think about the consequences of accidentally closing or breaking the urn.

Under the canopy where the moonlight fell around me in diffused patches, I concentrated on avoiding an ankle twist or a bone break or trampling on a venomous creature as we snaked around the trunks and skirted the ditches. If I got injured, my accomplice couldn't carry me to safety.

Eventually, we arrived at an opening of a tunnel. Although dark and threatening, I steadied the thumping of my heart and silenced the aching in my shoulder and back, and chased Djinn. It turned out to be a long road in the inky, crumbly, and moldy interiors, but we emerged in a copse mingled with shrubs, bordering a wheat field. The sun's first rays set the golden heads of the crop alight.

Djinn's eyes sparkled and danced. His smile was the widest I'd ever seen.

"Thank you for freeing me," he said.

"Are you sure we're safe? These lands aren't his?"

"Cheer up." Djinn pretended to tap my shoulder. "The world's yours now, and I'm your servant. If you accept me."

Relief should've flooded my being. Instead, I eyed him with suspicion. "Who's to say you won't do to me what you did to Bergamot?"

He studied me for a few moments.

"How can you forget the lullabies I sang to hush your crying, to make you fall asleep? Stories I told when you were lonely or sad? Who taught you to cook and do chores and educate you about the world outside? Yes, I was ordered to do so by Bergamot. But it was me who saw your pain and fear and isolation. I noticed how your heart swelled as you caressed the cats and watched the birds bathe in the water you changed daily for them. The tenderness in the touch as you cleansed the oxen and whispered in their ears. The songs you sang over the tedious, monotonous tasks of stirring the stew and washing the clothes on the stone. Your face never faltered even when purging the contents of Bergamot's piss pot."

He was right. He was always there, wordless, watching me, never angry, never judging.

"Equal to a . . . a father," he said.

His words startled me. But as I ruminated, I realized how patient he had been when I'd broken or burned things as he taught me different tasks. He never got bitter or disappointed, contrary to Bergamot's face dunked in constant displeasure. His language, mixed with patience, formed into gentle nudging and reminders and encouragements—identical to the way he had talked me into escaping this time. He had more parental qualities than the sum of Bergamot and his various possessions.

He watched me as if I was about to disavow the title he had dared to assume. But I appreciated him. His care moved me. He'd recognized the horrible future I had in store and had wheedled me—despite his selfish reasons—into heading toward a new destiny.

"I accept you as my attendant," I said. "But can I call you Cipher instead? In honor of the fresh start." The generic "Djinn" didn't fit him anymore. It was too distant and impersonal.

He grinned. "I will be loyal to you till the end of time. And you know my promises last unless—"

"Unless?"

"Unless you use your gift to destroy or age into Bergamot."

I held my hand near his heart. "Never."

He looked at the rising sun. "Now, where do you want to settle?"

I would miss my place on the hill. I sucked in a deep breath. But it was marvelous to own freedom. It would be an adventure from now, akin to the tales Djinn had narrated in my childhood.

"Not anywhere close to the horrible place you mentioned months ago. That city of Ashmere," I said. "But somewhere by a river, surrounded by greenery and friendly people." The papery seeds with their feathery bottom-up umbrellas came to my mind.

"I know just the place," he said, "and you will love it."

5

KITEMAKER'S BOY

"What are you doing, Orvin?" Edlyn approached the barn as I was about to bind the boy's legs to the chair.

Surprised, I turned around, shielding the furniture and its tenant with my body, glad that the gloominess outside didn't issue sufficient light to reach the corner of our windowless barn. Neither the fresh snow from last night nor the stinging cold had enough power to stall her from pursuing me. She was always intruding. Why couldn't she leave me alone?

Her silhouette at the threshold was enough to raise awareness of the thick and musty air lingering around me, reminding me of an expected responsibility I had left unfinished. Why did the rotting hay matter anymore? It wasn't like the animals were getting sick, feeding on it, or breathing in the mold. The horses were long dead, and so were the sheep.

I should have brought in a candle and closed the wide doors. Better to let her wonder about my whereabouts than lead her to me.

"Are you brewing trouble again?" Edlyn walked in, her boot heels crunching the gravel we'd laid two years ago to pack the dirt floor, her skirt swishing and sweeping the residual sawdust. "Wasn't stealing bread from our neighbors embarrassing enough? Their forgiveness saved us from a calamity."

I pressed my lips together at first, although silence became impossible. "You call this being saved from a calamity? Go to Dallin's Hollow at the grotto and ask him about it. See if he'll answer. Then go question our surviving son about how his gaunt body feels since he last ate the rabbit stew two weeks ago. I wish I had stolen before Dallin . . ." My chin trembled.

"Don't talk about Dallin in such manner, for goddesses' sake," she said. "Go hunting in the woods and see what you can bring home today. Staying here expecting to catch rats is useless. Rats only go where there is grain."

"Don't condemn me for the curse the kite brought."

A few weeks after the kite-flying festival this year, I had noticed a spot of red at the other end of my farm when I'd paused to wipe the sweat on my brow. The baked ground had hardened from a week of dry heat, making plowing arduous. No farmer embarked on such a foolish task since the ideal time was after the soil softened from the rain, but I had grown impatient from staring at the sky every day for a week and seeing no signs of clouds. I was also itching to plant my seeds.

The same restlessness made me stall my horse, drop the iron plow, and hasten to the curious object. In the bushes hemming my field rested a kite, guiltless and bright, its bridle and flying line limp and long. Time slowed. I forgot where I was or what I was doing. The discovery consumed me. It was my second time finding a kite, the first one being years ago on my father's land. Bitter and sour remnants of breakfast rose in my throat and gagged me. The ground sucked the strength from my legs, and I thudded like a sack of potatoes.

"Orvin!" Edlyn stepped deeper into the barn with her hands on her hips and a frown on her face.

Why did she fling out my name the way she did? All wrapped up in the hardness of a rock, the strictness of a schoolteacher, and the condemnation of a judge. It made me recoil each time, giving her ample reason to disbelieve me.

"Why are you here?" she said. "You should be out on the mountain."

Since summer, she had done nothing but complain and badger me to scout for more food. From where was I to get more food? She was aware our soil was dead from the curse that had ridden on the backs of the kite. All our endeavors at planting seeds failed. Not a single seedling sprouted. Even the earthworms hadn't survived. The rains could have worked their usual charm, but not this growing season, not on our land; they forsook us, too. By this time of the year, our barns should have been full of harvest waiting to be threshed during the winter. Alas, misfortune had settled over us and our property, and we had to endure it for a year from the day of the kite's sighting.

"What I'm attempting to do is to keep us alive. Why don't you try bartering something?" I stood in place, afraid to move.

"We have nothing left to barter. Unless you want me to barter *you*." She glared at me, waiting for me to concede. "I'm weary of the same old argument with you. When will you understand?"

By "understand," she meant yielding to her demands.

"Six more months, Orvin. Until then, stay with trying to find something edible from the forest. All these other things you pursue bring nothing but more trouble."

"There are no animals in the mountain forests. They're all hunted out." Woods, woods, woods; it was no bother for her to work her mouth and send me off to the woods, except we weren't the only family to set snares. People grew their grains and vegetables but also craved some game, regardless of whether they were accursed. After the first snowfall, the squirrels and hares went into hibernation. Did she even know how clever they were at hiding? How their fur matched with the surroundings? I had gotten lucky with that rabbit.

And oh, the drudgery of plodding up and down the mountain, staying still for hours, and struggling to discern the scurrying notes of the animals underneath the wailing winds. Hunting involved unpleasant attempts to set traps while producing the least amount of disturbance.

Foraging for burrows was no better either. It was a long process, and it numbed both my hands and my brain.

"But what about fruits and mushrooms?" I could almost hear her assert. Easy for her to say when all she did was sit by the hearth, basking in the warmth of the crackling wood—the wood I labored to chop as I endured the elements outside. Trees bearing apples and pears and the berry-producing shrubs were few and scattered among the trees, and the villagers picked them clean long before the fruits even ripened. So, she shouldn't expect me to get those. But as far as mushrooms were concerned, perhaps I should send her out scouting without telling her they appeared only in the fall. Maybe she would find the wrong kind, helping us end our sorry existence.

"Then how did you find the rabbit for the last—what is behind you, Orvin?"

She advanced fast to investigate. I strode across the barn to shove her out the entrance. Famine and hunger on our property hadn't tempered her strength or her will. She forced her way past me and stood in front of my captive. I could have pulled her arm and dragged her out, but I had never given power to my impulses. Besides, she would gouge my eyes out if I used violence with her.

"Human flesh now, Orvin? Are you that lazy to hunt?"

"Go back to the house." She loved interfering, didn't she? How stupid was she to think I intended to eat him?

This curse had made the community sever its ties with us—as we all did to those who were served the curse—because if someone helped out of kindness, the curse beset them. So begging and borrowing were not viable remedies. Thieving and bartering worked, but once people knew about the kite, they became wary of any association. And they would know because the blighted had to declare the kite at the entrance of their property soon after they discovered it. But hunting had no adverse consequences. So, Edlyn had gone to extremes regarding the activity.

Although, I had a plan.

"Untie him and return the boy to his family!" Her shoulders were firm like her face, and her eyes angered. "I cannot believe you have stooped to this level."

"He is not an ordinary boy." Even though the boy was about the same age as our ten-year-old Dallin, with similarly colored hair and skin, I cared little about . . . I don't know why I compared this creature with my dead son because the one in front of me, his family, his clan, was the one responsible for Dallin's death.

"Look at him! He's wasting away of flesh, worse than Wynton," she said with concern.

She kneeled beside the chair and lifted the boy's matted hair from his wide-set eyes and crooked nose with the same touch she showed our sons, Dallin and Wynton. I didn't like what she was doing. He didn't deserve it.

"What is your name, child?" she asked in a soft voice.

The boy kept his gaze on the ground.

"You don't need to know his name." If she could understand my intention and agree with it, we wouldn't need to suffer for the remaining half of the year. Surely she would see some wisdom in it. "He is a kitemaker's child."

"A Kimakar? You kidnapped a Kimakar clan's child?" Her features transformed as he rose to confront me—a ferocious animal poised to attack the hunter. "Your foolishness knows no bounds." Her hands balled into fists. "It's bad enough their families are blamed for misfortunes and they're imprisoned within a compound surrounded by a tall wall, all because of fearmongers like you. But this? This is going too far."

"Exaggeration isn't necessary, Edlyn. Kimakars can farm, keep cattle, and do everything inside the walls. They are treated better by some people than we are. So it's not a prison. Have you ever been to prison?"

"If you don't get your act together, *you* will soon land in one." She wagged her finger in my face.

"People dislike Kimakars," I said. "They have become the root of unhappiness and suffering of the villagers."

"Save the hateful sermon for the sinful and the skeptics. You have been given eyes, but what you see is entirely different."

I would not let her overpower me. The curse had bereaved me of my first child; I would not let it do the same to my younger one.

"Release him right now!" she said.

"For once, I will not listen to you." I put as much determination in my voice as I could.

"Tying him like this and killing him to fill your belly will not reverse your ruin," she said.

"I don't intend to kill him." What a foolish woman. "Maybe make him starve like us to show him what their curses are like. After all, kites never land on their houses or properties."

"Properties? Kimakars own nothing, and whatever they own is hand-outs. Their life's purpose is doing God Vavajod's work." She whimpered as she set eyes on the boy again. "Look at him. He's a skeleton, and you intend to starve him?" She swore under her breath and got on her knees to release the cloth fastenings pinning the boy's wrists to the chair. "Goddesses only know how the Kimakars are surviving within the walls. Such isolation . . ." Her nimble fingers undid the knots I had tightened with my knobby ones. "I'm tired of your ways, Orvin. How long did you wait outside their walls seeking to lure him? How would you feel if someone enticed Wynton and snatched him?"

"I found him digging the ground in the forest. Look at his fingers if you don't believe me." Why did I have to provide proof of my actions to her? Other families in our village of Diskit had accommodating wives, like our neighbor Cerelia, who worshipped her husband Alcott Millard and obeyed his word. Edlyn had been such. And sweet, too, when I had brought her violets in our youth and proposed to her, but she had developed a high-handed manner after our hardship had begun six months ago.

"I aim to release him later." Not let him walk away the way she wanted me to, but if I got word around to his clan about his capture, they would get worried and offer me a bribe for his release. I could ask for grains, or maybe meat. Why not both? And if misfortune fell on them for helping me, then so be it. They deserved to sample the affliction they dispensed to others.

"How many years have you been flying kites on Kite-Flying Day, Orvin?"

What kind of question was that? What was she attempting to teach me now? I clenched my jaw.

The thought of the yearly ritual was distasteful. The village accorded far too much significance to the day and the people involved, giving more credence to the beliefs and practices than needed, making a useless fuss.

I had been part of it once. My chest had filled with spiritual obligation and pride as I'd volunteered for the formidable task of being a drummer. The residents of Diskit considered a surrender to the duties of a drummer to be the ultimate pious act.

On the first calendar day of summer, I was celebrated along with other drummers. Cooks prepared and served us a hearty breakfast to strengthen their bodies, and afterward the priests engaged us in a long ceremonial farewell. Handmade garlands of roses adorned our necks, perfuming the air, stirring excitement in the onlookers. No prayers were left unsaid. No songs were left unsung.

Then we climbed to the Drummer's Plateau—an outcropping jutting out at midheight of Mount Katahorn—with large drums on our backs and enough food and water to last weeks. It took us a day and a half through maple- and conifer-forested slopes to our destination. To trudge uphill on the rocky and uneven ground was a feat, harsh enough to shake the wills of those whose faith faltered. Still, as history shows, not one of us ever abandoned our task.

Once we reached the spot, we erected and lived in temporary lodgings, waiting for Gatra—the first lot of summer winds, sent forth by God Vavajod. Those winds arose once a year from behind the Meltwater Mountain Range—Mount Katahorn being one of its highest peaks—clipped its tallest crests and plunged toward the plateau. Sweeping across the flattened outcropping, they turned upward again, high above the village.

The boy's right arm was free, and Edlyn labored at the left.

"What are you standing there for? Loosen his feet," she said.

I didn't budge. My head was filled with visions: the excitement racing our hearts at the smallest sign of Gatra, drum skins vibrating from our sticks pounding against them day and night, the pain and weariness sinking deeper and deeper into our muscles and bones, and our disregard for it for seven days until the Kite-Flying Day.

Our calls were so powerful. The sounds rumbled down to the village, rebounding among the houses, signaling an urgency, declaring the approach of an important day. Now though, the beats served me headaches. They reminded me of thunder, awakening a nervousness that, like lightning, the calamity could strike anyone and anywhere, just like it had befallen my father's family in my childhood, just like it had mine. What guarantee was there that it wouldn't appear a third time? Perhaps right after we carried through this harrowing year.

"You focus too much on the calamities," Edlyn said. "The kites help answer our prayers and wishes too. If both are dispensed by the kites and calamities appear far less in proportion, how can you blame the Kimakars? They do nothing more than make kites for the village. They even heave them up the plateau for us to write our prayers on the paper sail and wooden spine and send them flying as an offering to our god." She caressed the boy's chin. "Be warned, Orwin. Nothing good comes out of offending Vavajod and tarnishing the sacredness of the Kimakar clan."

I peered outside the barn doors.

Since I was born, I'd never missed a Kite-Flying Day ceremony until the end of the ruinous year that had befallen our family. My parents had thought our household of three had survived the crisis unscathed. What was not to celebrate? The ordeal had reaffirmed their devotion, doubling it even. But for me, the opposite became the truth. After the kites had flown on the Drummer's Plateau, I evaded the activities and snuck back to the village. It would have been shameful if the villagers detected my transgression, but I had lost my faith and had no desire to stay any longer.

In my father's case, a blue kite had rested by the stairs of the tavern he owned, whose second floor housed our residence. Before I found it, I had never seen tears stain my father's cheeks. But with his head high, he prayed with us for strength to overcome our long impending trial. Then he went out and hung the kite on a stake by the stairs.

Not one of our neighbors patronized our tavern during that year of the curse. I helped empty many, many containers of ale gone bad. And even though it was away from our house, we smelled it day and night, continually reminding us of our adversity. We'd had less than crumbs to eat then, similar to what Wynton, Edlyn, and I had now.

My parents had remained staunch in their conviction, but they had twenty years of wisdom above me. For a sixteen-year-old, six years over my buried son, the painful pangs in the abdomen and the severe isolation were unbearable; my life felt like the wick of a melted candle—burned and useless. It stopped me from going up Mount Katahorn altogether.

Edlyn gawked at me with an intention I didn't understand. I studied the lines on her face: the years had been kinder to her than to me. Would she have married me if she had known about my lack of enthusiasm and attendance at the Kite-Flying Day?

She exhaled and focused on my foe. The boy was odd; he sat motionless despite the freedom from the bonds, shivering under his clothes. I hadn't noticed the wear and tear and the meagerness of his attire before. It was insufficient for the weather outside.

"We can't let him go," I said to Edlyn. "This is an opportunity nobody's ever had before."

"I will not partake in your sins. Return him to his clan *now*."

I closed my eyes for a moment before I returned my attention to the boy.

"What do they call you?" Edlyn asked my captive. She slipped her shawl from her shoulders and wrapped it around his upper body and head, leaving a lock of gold visible.

The boy shifted his gaze to her feet, not meeting hers. "Lawley Kimakar."

"Why were you digging in the woods, Lawley?" When he didn't answer, she continued, "Was it for your family? How long have you been away from them? They must be worried."

Her statement brought no emotion to his face.

E dlyn had talked me into doing what she wanted. I was the head of my homestead; however, her domineering nature had made me such a namby-pamby. Living with her was getting unbearable, and I'm sure others observed her behavior and sided with me in silence. Can't a man have a moment to himself without being pursued every second and questioned about every action? I thought of our world's past. What must have the men undergone when the four goddesses ended the treacherous era of the disgraceful gods and uplifted the women of Sigilis Septerra, and culturally, morally and socially made them as powerful as men, if not more? Did those men feel what I felt now?

"Stop wriggling your hand." I was curt with the boy. We were on our way to his home, his wrist in my grip. "Quit lagging."

Why couldn't he listen to me? It wasn't like he was deaf.

"Will you stop it?" I raised my voice.

What was I doing, following Edlyn's orders? The road we were on threw a loop toward the forest, and I studied the tree trunks as we progressed; most were large, but I eyed one narrow enough to suit my purpose. The bottom of my shirt could make sturdy bindings.

The boy rolled his wrist as if he had gotten a whiff of my thoughts and, with a quick jerk, escaped. Stunned, I turned to watch his movements through the brush. When sense took over my mind, I followed him. To let him escape would be a mistake.

I spotted him several paces ahead to my right, so I changed direction. Then I saw him to my left. He was fast, and before long, he was unnoticeable, and with the twigs and leaves and people's tracks soiling the snow, it was impossible to track him. The wind had picked up. Soon it would start howling as it made its way through the trees, and it would be a while before the gales died again. Lack of food made me tire easily. I stopped to rest and listen for his footsteps—no crunch over the quickening wind.

What was the likelihood of Edlyn believing in this state of affairs?

There was no way I could let an opportunity as rare as this fade, because six more months of hopelessness were unendurable. I was afraid it would end one of our lives, if not more.

I was on the smaller plateau we called Plugus, a place of lesser reverence than Drummer's Plateau but important to those who weren't unable to reach the higher one and wanted to participate in the holiday festivities. I breathed in the sharp winter air and pried through the understory of thickets, hoping to find the Kimakar. Nothing ever went right when a kite flown on Kite-Flying Day floated to your home.

We had left the homestead at noon; it was past midafternoon now, and soon the skies would darken, making the trip back through the rocky, snow-covered slopes dangerous. Also, going home empty-handed was a bad idea. What would I tell Edlyn? I would be in the same circumstance as I had been before I had stumbled upon the boy and brought him to the barn.

My heart jumped just as he stepped into the clearing. He was about to take a rest, but upon detecting me, his eyes widened, and panic spread across his face.

I spurted in his direction. He scurried hither and thither to find a suitable hiding spot but yelped when he realized the lack of them, causing him to bolt farther into the area between the forested slopes we had come from and the steep, craggy uprising of Mount Katahorn.

I stalked him, blocking him from climbing higher toward the Drummer's Plateau, then from retracing his way to the woods. I had no intention of losing him to the trees again. But he didn't stop. Instead, he ran right over the edge.

A shock of horror slashed through me. I froze, staring at the brink of the plateau and the mountain beside it. What made him more afraid of me than falling to his death? The behavior was most peculiar. And why had he done such a thing when I proposed to take him to his village? He couldn't have figured out my motive before he'd escaped my grip.

I muddled to the brink and found him hanging off a tree growing some way down along the decline. How would I remedy this state of perplexity? I went on my belly and stretched my hand, but he was beyond my reach. He clasped the branch with both hands, his knuckles as pale as the white beans I grew on my farm. And although his eyes were brimming with dread and he repeatedly cast them at the depth below, they didn't express relief at my extended hand. Nor did he plead for rescue.

"Is that you, Orvin?" It was my neighbor.

"Everything is fine." I sprang up. "I . . . I just lost my cap." I brushed my fingers through my hair. It had grayed from months of dour statements from Edlyn. "The gusts are strong."

"What are you doing here?" Alcott asked.

My tyrannical woman had sent Alcott to keep me on track. Why couldn't Alcott Millard and his wife, Cerelia, sit on their pile of grains and flour and bread, eat it, grow stout, and keep to themselves? I bet they were stealing from the villagers who went to get their grains ground at their mill, the crops the poor villagers had grown through hard labor. And it wasn't easy work cultivating on these mountain lands, under the influence of the moody mountain weather.

"Did you see the Kimakar child anywhere?" Alcott asked.

I narrowed my eyes at him.

"He ran away from home, the poor soul. Many found him digging, searching for roots or mushrooms to eat," Alcott said.

Of course, how else would I have garnered enough courage and conceived a plot to snatch him?

"Why would he run away when the villagers fulfilled the needs of the kitemakers?" I asked.

"Orvin, you know they don't have everything. They're poor. Locked behind walls because a few powerful and bitter villagers held them responsible for the curses that sailed with the kites." He looked at me as though he was trying to change my beliefs. "They do nothing but make kites. Innocent. As far as the boy is concerned, he's special. Cerelia and I wanted to feed and shelter him before the wrong people caught and tormented him."

I didn't appreciate his haughty manner of talking. He should have married Edlyn.

"If you see him, will you bring him to my mill?" he said.

Why? So he could reap the reward from the Kimakars? I wanted Alcott gone.

"That Kimakar boy needs the most help," he said while descending the slope toward the forest's margin.

And my Wynton, who had witnessed his elder brother's demise, didn't need any? Oh, but Alcott wouldn't want to give his charity to us because then he would get tangled in our curse's suffering.

"The Kimakars loathe the boy and made his life difficult. They think he is interfering with Vavajod's wishes." Alcott was already in the woods, swerving the tree trunks.

My ears perked up.

"How?" I called after him.

"He can undo curses, Jaja Orvin!" Alcott was far, hidden by the trees. "He can break them!"

I stilled the moment I heard him shout the sentence. Had my ears heard right?

"The boy can undo curses," I repeated.

An urgency blossomed in me such that my breath ran ragged and my heart thumped, and I flew to the edge. The boy had to be saved. I would give him anything he wanted, even listen to Edlyn. My knees drove to the ground first, then my front side hit the dirt. I had to rescue the boy, for Wynton's sake. But as I threw my hand toward the tree, the urgency distorted into dread and lodged in my throat and chest.

The boy wasn't hanging by the branch anymore. He was gone.

T he curse had pillaged our prospects. I knew we began the year after Kite-Flying Day with nothing, but an assurance of fortunate days ahead had slipped through my fingers before I grabbed it.

I was still on the plateau when it got dark, and I didn't dare to return to my wretched home. Huddling within my coat, I tucked my body in a cluster of bushes to shelter from the raw elements and closed my eyes. The possibilities of what could have been came to me, and I reveled in the marvelous spectacle throughout the night.

A cackle and flap of wings awoke me at dawn. Ahead of me, a turkey swooped to the ground from the low branch of a tree. The cackling turned to putting, and soon I had a dead bird over my shoulder.

Younger Edlyn would have given me affection for my effort and a smile worth a bag of diamonds and taafeites, but upon arriving home, what I heard was, "About time you showed yourself. Get the fire going in the hearth."

She assumed I had returned the Kimakar boy, and not wanting to break her version of reality, I did as I was told. The turkey stew was the best meal in months, but instead of gathering our family around our supper table, Edlyn ate hers with Wynton behind closed doors in our sleeping quarters.

From that day on, she spent most of her days and nights there, unless she had chores to do. I didn't inquire, and she didn't explain her altered habits. I wasn't interested in why she took bowls of food in and brought empty ones out, why she took buckets of clean, warm water in and returned with dirty, and why she wasted water in washing clothes often. The arrangement suited me; fewer demands and tart remarks fell on my ears. Who didn't prefer being spared from humiliation?

For that week, I stayed in bed long after the sun rose. Relief from Edlyn's demands was liberating. I cleared the hay from the barn, spread it out on the dead land, chopped wood, and even chased and captured a wild pheasant and a squirrel. Yet it wasn't enough. The loneliness got to me, and I missed my son.

"Can I talk to Wynton?" I asked Edlyn when she stepped out of the sleeping quarters and locked them behind her.

A sudden chill of apprehension drove through me. I searched for distress in her eyes and for darkness around them, something to hint at Wynton's state of being, but I found none. She could mask her emotions and control her will with exactness.

"I don't want him to learn your ways, Orwin."

"What does he do inside all day? The sun will do him good."

"Then why don't you go bask in it? Maybe it will knock some kindness and forbearance into you," she said.

What did she think I had been doing since the red kite had landed on our land? She was the one who was blind to my patience and self-control.

In the following days, I stole glimpses of the space beyond, in between her comings and goings. My fear kept strengthening until the day my tolerance ran out. I resolved to intrude, even if she disallowed my admittance. It was my house.

Except Edlyn was too bright for me. She guessed my intention and refrained from approaching the door until I blocked her way.

"What do you want, Orwin?"

"I want to see Wynton." He was my son too, and Edlyn had no right holding him hostage.

"Go to the woods to—"

"Good morning!" Alcott chimed in the entryway.

Edlyn, noting my distraction, sneaked into the sleeping quarters.

I stood guard at the front door, frowning, studying the heavy tray of bread and cheese and grapes Alcott was balancing in his hands. Cerelia was closing the gate of my property in the distance, trailing him. Finally, they showed some kindness. But the extended smile pasted on Alcott's face idled too long, and I became skeptical of his motives.

"May I come in to offer my congratulations?" Alcott said.

"What for?" I refused to return his gaiety.

"Did you, by any chance, find your cap the other day?" he asked.

Was the scoundrel trying to trap me in my lie? I lowered my eyes at the source of the rising aroma: yeasty, earthy, like stepping into the forest after the rain. Saliva gathered in my mouth.

"Where is everyone? Edlyn? Wynton?" Cerelia, in her bright green outfit and high-spirited voice, was too cheerful for me. At a different time, the wine jug she carried would have enticed me, but at present I mainly wanted to get inside the forbidden room.

"I knew it had happened as soon as I saw the birds flying on your land and settling on your trees," Cerelia said.

Birds? I couldn't bear the Millards in my house. Edlyn should entertain them, not me, and I should be with Wynton instead. Maybe an untamed fever had gripped my son's body, making him sweat, drenching the covers, or perhaps his energy had ebbed like Dallin on his deathbed. I couldn't let my second son die without seeing his face.

The small amount of fear that had stepped into me when I'd pegged the red kite at the entrance of our property, and which had taken permanent residence during the last six months, livened up, burgeoned out of proportion, and broke its confinement.

I crashed against the door.

Cerelia gasped.

"Jaja Orwin!" Alcott said. "What has come over you?"

Nothing was going to hinder me. I bashed my shoulder on the wood for the second time. Cerelia screamed, followed by a clattering noise behind me. Shards of glass and globs of liquid landed on my body as the door ahead of me broke open, and I stumbled toward the lit fireplace. I saw Edlyn hunched over the cot, holding Wynton's hand.

I thrust her aside to get to my son.

"Pah." I heard Wynton's voice in the opposite corner.

I found him behind me, cowering in the space between the other bed and the wall. My head snapped back to the first bed. Now sitting, with his feet touching the floor, was the kitemaker's boy: clean hair and skin, clothed warmly, and calm.

"I knew you found him, Jaja Orwin!" Alcott walked into the room. "But I had to see him for myself."

What was this? More tricks from the Kimakar? I *had* seen the boy go over the edge, hang against the cliff, and then vanish. How had he . . .? No one else had ventured to the elevation, except for Alcott's brief intrusion. My confusion cleared as I noted the scratches and the slashes on his face, limbs, and joints, and the salve gleaming on them and the ongoing healing underneath. As unbelievable as it was, the boy had descended the rock's steep and cutting surface to save his life and sought safety in Edlyn's arms.

Images of Edlyn slaving over the tub scrubbing additional clothes, of her pounding the mortar and pestle that drove me mad, and of shoulders stooped under the weights of the extra buckets as she scurried from the well to the house burst into my mind.

"Jubilation! The curse is over!" Cerelia said as Wynton slid next to the boy.

The situation became clear to me then. Edlyn had placed distance between the Kimakar and me as she had tended the boy. And in gratitude, the boy had destroyed the curse, probably the very night she had sheltered him. How could I have missed the signs: the boon of the turkey in the copse, the pheasant and the squirrel, the parting of the gloom, the birds, and the Millards' arrival with food?

My wife's posture was lit with contentment and peace. I took notice of the acceptance and kinship sealed in the firm grip of hands between the two boys; I saw the honesty in my neighbors' glee. And when I allowed my gaze to hover over the boy, I found no animosity or fear but the most gracious of smiles I had ever seen on a child's face.

Nevertheless, he was a Kimakar—his clan was the source of my woes, not once, but twice. His people had cost me my innocence and faith, but above all, my Dallin. How can a father overcome the loss of a child?

The boy's smile wavered—the way Dallin's did when he tried to convince me the trouble he had stirred was of no consequence.

The boy before me was a child too, like my Dallin. A runaway who had been digging into the frozen ground with his fingers. He had been hungry, cold, and afraid. What suffering had he endured that he had preferred to descend a towering rock face and risk death than being returned home?

And to think my hardships—lasting twelve months years ago and six months now—were terrible. For how many years had he endured his distress? As long as his people had known about his ability, was my guess.

In one swift moment, our unfinished year of ruin flashed before me: a time when a red kite had swooped down and chosen our farmland as its ultimate resting place, causing our livestock to die and our land to wither, and our eldest's demise. I had suffered months of hunger and frustration and blamed everyone and everything, the Kimakars in particular. I had wallowed in constant spite and anger. It had changed me.

But not Edlyn.

My cheeks stung with shame. As though the curse wasn't evil enough, I had worsened the circumstances by serving nothing but foulness and disagreements to Edlyn and Wynton. The Kimakar boy had revoked the harm hovering over my loved ones. He had changed our future overnight.

I caught the innocence in the boy's wide-set eyes and his crooked nose. The gold of his hair reminded me so much of my long-gone first child.

"Lawley." I acknowledged his name for the first time and stretched my hand out to him. "Let's remove the kite."

A grin lit Edlyn's face, the kind she used to shower me with during our courtship—adoring and filled with kindness. Its absence had been so prolonged, I had forgotten its existence and had not missed it. Hope behind her eyes and her dovelike affection warmed me more than a seat by the fireside and melted my resentfulness against her. I took a step forward and hugged her.

Wynton, Lawley, and I buried the kite's skeleton—just as my father and I had—by the gate that had displayed it for over half a year. When we finished, the group locked their hands against their hearts, bowed their heads, and murmured prayers in thanks to Vavajod. But I didn't join them, not yet. I squeezed the children's hands and thanked them instead.

6

No Ordinary Bargain

Anum

C andles and lanterns were not the problem, but the fire their wicks carried was the real issue.

"Je Anum, did you hear me?" Lady Primeveire said. "Snuff them out and come help me with some decisions."

I had heard her; in fact, I perceived her so well that my body welded to her bedchamber chair and a familiar impairment seeped into my limbs. I couldn't help but delay Lady Primeveire's command, stall my inevitable misery. In a short time, the weakness would capture my emotions and overpower my sensibility. This distress of the flames never left me. How could it when my lady's habit rekindled it again and again by always directing *me* to extinguish the candles and the lanterns?

The other four ladies-in-waiting hid their half-suppressed, unseemly laughs behind their handkerchiefs as they followed Lady Primeveire into the drawing room. Why did they even bother with those embroidered pieces of linen and silk? They knew I was aware of their tricks, of being the source of their entertainment, and of them encouraging me to undertake socially unacceptable deeds for their amusement and to get me in trouble. I was no fool.

I glanced out the other door, hoping to snag a maid, but the hallway was empty, just as the chamber I occupied. This candle-snuffing affair to save overuse of candles was a new obsession of hers. One shouldn't worry about hoarding money when the back door of the safe was bleeding gold crowns and silver spards. The new jewels in her hair themselves could have bought several candle manufactories and their corresponding candle storehouses. Windrage, they could have purchased charmed sorghum pellets and their special lanterns to brighten the Manor for a year instead of trifling with pitiful lighting for the vast rooms and hallways, the corners of which were always shrouded in shadows, whether night or day.

Five fat candles of the candelabra dripped wax on the decorative sconce holding them. Their flames flickered. The elaborate array of dangling crystals underneath reflected them, multiplying the flares manifold, sending my heart banging against my ribs. Willing strength into my knees, I pushed against the chair and got up.

The women tracked my moves, and the moment I fled toward the door to find help, they flocked to Her Ladyship, whispering. Winning our mistress' favors was their game, and I was their pawn. With examples of such behavior, why would I ever make them my confidants?

"Je Anum!" my lady said.

My body turned rigid.

"How long will it take you?" she said. "Je Odelia, go help her." She waved her hand at the lady-in-waiting closest to her.

My desperation amused Odelia too much to assist, but she made a show of gathering the skirts of her expansive silk dress.

I glanced at the flames once more. They swayed at the slightest whiff of breeze, the scantiest movement in the air surrounding them. They staged such innocence. Except they concealed such insatiable hunger! One unassuming candle sitting too close to the curtains was all it had taken to convert our home into a bonfire. The same greed hid in the brightness topping the candles on Lady Primeveire's side table. Their tameness was so deceitful. They were clever creatures, opportunists, bidding their time. Then, when a flame got its chance, it embodied its true ravenous form. Puffing plumes of smoke and roaring, the monster thrilled at torching and scorching everything in sight.

I shuddered.

Why had my mother trusted me with the candle that night? I closed my eyes and swallowed.

My mother's screams of "fire" . . . the brilliance, nighttime simulating daytime . . . the smoke choking and blinding me as I pulled my brother behind me, sensing each step of the stairs with my hand . . .

I wanted to run, escape the memory, do anything to stop it, but I was paralyzed. My heart thumped, each pulse swooshing in the hollow between my clavicles.

The suffocating heat . . . the roaring and the crackling all around . . .

The blaze licking and devouring the walls, the furniture, the books, the food . . . closing in as we inched toward the exit . . .

With a cough and a shaking hand, I snatched the snuffer. It had to be done, so I shut my mind to sinister thoughts and made haste. Yet I sweated, and my feet slipped inside my shoes as I proceeded.

The burgeoning dread loosening my bladder . . .

My brother coughing, struggling to drag in a breath . . .

One, two, three, four, five. I choked the flames rapidly until the odor of the burned wicks crossed my nostrils. The snuffer dropped from my hands, clattering against the stone floor. I cringed and backed away in quick steps, the sound of my heartbeat now thrashing in my ears. The doomful day of my past . . .

The stench of singed hair and flesh as the neighbors rescued and smothered my brother and me in quilts . . . the horrible reek of the partially charred remains of my sister and father . . .

A feeble whimper slipped through my trembling lips. And as I pressed my hands on my abdomen and resisted an urge to vomit, a maid scurried into the room and offered rescue. Was it the snuffer that had alerted her? I cared little. She guided me to a nearby stool and offered me a goblet, the water sloshing because of my unsteady grip. And had she not aided me to drink, the vessel would have tumbled and dented, flinging its contents much to Lady Primeveire's displeasure. The velvet curtains, the ornate wall molding and paneling of gold and white, the central rug from the Khand region of Terra Three, rare, round and lush, and the floral chair were more precious in Ashmere than human life.

While I avoided gazing at the cause of my distress, how could I escape the sickly, stomach-churning odor of death, no matter how faint, when it was in the very air I breathed? Yet I grabbed the sides of the stool to calm my nerves and continued breathing. When somewhat recovered, I wiped the spilled tears, smoothed my clothes, and then walked into the drawing room with my head high.

Nothing escaped Her Ladyship's flock of attendants, even though the maid had done her best to shield my plight. They smirked and leered at me with such self-satisfaction as if they had triumphed over me at a tournament. How I wished for a friend, a comforter, someone I could share my anguish with and who offered no judgment.

No sooner had I perched myself on the chair near my lady's chaise longue she sighed.

"You have yet to be successful in any task I allocate you," she said to me. "Isn't it right?"

It was a lie. How could I have been with Lady Primeveire for ten years and not accomplished any tasks? Arguing or refuting was a transgression, unless I wanted to be scandalized and expelled.

Besides, why did she get pleasure out of focusing on me? I wasn't the youngest or the newest of the group. Did she perceive a shortfall she wished to remedy? Or could it be because I was different? I was, in so many ways. Being from the highlands of the continent of Terra Three, which was disagreeable in itself, my skin was fair, unlike their shades of brown, rich in color and luster. My voice was harsh and unpliable to my lady's demands for melodic singing. And sometimes, my training in decorum and language slipped to reveal hints of the non-noble station of my birth—a secret that, if exposed, could condemn me. On occasions, I wondered why, out of the vast selection of ladies, she had chosen *me*. Then again, why did she prefer younger ladies-in-waiting to the wisdom and experience of older ones?

"I need one of you to arrange travel to the witch for new charmed blankets," my lady said, placing a grape in her mouth from the plate her companions held for her.

Distress flashed on everyone's faces at the mention of the witch and the task, but the emotion dissipated before our mistress could discover it.

"One for me and one for Timothea. Poor dear, life has become so burdensome for her since her beau perished from poisoning." She squashed another grape between her teeth. "One of you, cover my feet. Why can't I ever get the chill out of them?"

They all rushed to be the first to secure the shawl and drape it over her legs. I should have followed because our lady noted such behavior or, should I say, the lack of it, except I hadn't yet regained my composure from candle-snuffing. Besides, another reason existed that I dared not breathe life into, one whose acknowledgment implied digging my grave or wiping out my future. Yet the notions seeped into my thoughts more often nowadays than I permitted them. And as I observed my coddled, lazy mistress, they reappeared: the boredom with the fixed routine day after day; the fatigue of attending to Lady Primeveire's endless complaints and demands; the maddening, meaningless talks in the same old bedchamber and drawing room; and lack of liberty of time for myself. And, of course, her tendency of singling me out time after time to extinguish her candles and lanterns, whether out of habit or to derive entertainment from my misery. For Father Bhumi's sake, I couldn't stop those thoughts. I let the corrupt feelings sweep in and possess me, and I finally admitted to the dissatisfaction I harbored toward my mistress and the Manor life. I could leave, but where would I go? What would I do? If only there was something or someone else to distract me, arouse hope, make my life bearable.

"How far is it?" one of the ladies-in-waiting said.

"The village of Memora? Where Her Ladyship wants us to go?" another said. "It's a quarter way up a mountain in the Meltway Mountain Range, so . . . three to four months."

"You don't have to be in the coach the entire time," my lady said to no one in particular. "Manor houses and homes of those sympathetic to the overlord's cause abound along the way."

"Then the travel would take even longer," Odelia said.

"Are you grumbling?" A hint of irritation and sternness surfaced in Lady Primeveire's face.

"Of course not, Your Ladyship," Odelia said, pasting enthusiasm on her face. "The travel should be effortless and dealing with the witch easy. The mountain air would do us good."

Ashmere Manor was cloaked in pretense, smiles being the most popular. The insincerity served one purpose: servile obedience and excessive eagerness to please the nobles. Everyone—from the servants to the beekeepers, the footmen to the ladies-in-waiting—who lived or set foot in the Manor was guilty of it. I was one of them. But much to my disadvantage, it was another element of my life vexing me. How short-sighted had I been to aspire to this kind of life through my childhood?

"Now, if you use the official mainway and catch a gleam-flash, you'll be there in a month," Her Ladyship said. "Take enough food if you decide to do so. You won't be able to get off the gleam-flash once you're swept away by it. Unless, of course, it peters out."

"Gleam-flashes can be occasionally unreliable in many ways," one of the recently hired said. "But my father swore by it."

The others frowned at her for bringing the subject of her family into the conversation as if their status equaled Her Ladyship's, but the topic evaded my lady's scrutiny as her mind was on gleam-flashes; she continued, "You'll have to double back if it shoots past your destination and lands you in a forsaken corner somewhere."

The rest of us expressed our agreement.

"Je Anum will go," my lady said, her finger raised in decisive force.

I gulped my spit. Was she testing me again? I could never be sure if she had learned something unpalatable about me. A mistress should be benevolent, with high moral values, but mine lacked those qualities. She scrutinized us to find faults in our personalities and behavior and the transgressions we committed for the sole purpose of applying it to her advantage. She relished gossip as Odelia did the desserts. And paired with her inclination to use rumors as weapons to destroy a person, she was one powerful noblewoman.

An air of relief hung over the others. These ladies-in-waiting were supposed to be my friends, assisting one another as sisters did, but their smugness and sneers told another story. If I could swipe their sly smiles off their snotty faces they so pampered and prettied with creams and pigmented powders, I would do so with glee. Except I was supposed to be a proper lady. My fingernails bit into my palms.

"Do you have any issue with travel and fulfilling your duty, Je Anum?" my lady said.

Plenty, I wanted to snap. One, my primary responsibility was to tend to her rooms and her wardrobe. None of which involved traveling to foreign lands. Two, correspondence—reading letters to Her Ladyship and writing on her behalf—besides relaying messages upon command was Odelia's duty. Three was my lack of experience outside the boundaries of Ashmere Manor. I'd embarked on a long journey just twice, and one of them had gone horribly wrong. And for four, the glaring reason: the idea of meeting the witch was beyond distressing. A witch to me was a person short on patience, easy to offend, quick to anger, and a curse-caster. Why couldn't she send a messenger? But my lady was not a person to back down once she made a decision.

"No trouble at all, Your Ladyship. It will be my utmost pleasure." As I directed stony stares at the other ladies-in-waiting, I tumbled into a chasm on the inside, blindfolded yet aware of the terror that was to come. "Do you need anything else from her?"

"Secure me blankets in the same colors she sent before." Lady Primeveire yawned. "And instruct her to use the same magic spell again."

I agreed with deceptive zeal and abandoned the drawing room under the guise of preparations. In reality, I was still shaken from before and newly irritated and uneasy about the impending assignment. It made me twitch. Who was she going to transfer my current responsibilities to in my absence?

"Ugh!" I forced my fists onto my temples, hard enough to cause pain, once I was out of hearing distance. "This is unbelievable. Unreal, unreal, unreal."

I needed to move, pace, and release the pressure building in my nerves so my steps took me toward my bedchamber. I was also nursing grudges and was terrified that my veneer of benevolence was about to crack. A torrent of harsh words was held back solely by a limp veil of will, and I did *not* want them to be unleashed in her lady's drawing room. Imagine the horror. If only I had a confidant with receptive ears and a kind heart!

"If only, if only," I said to myself. "How irrational. Do you think you're holding a djinn's urn? To wish for such a person is a fool's dream."

Upon returning to my bedchamber, I slumped against the pillows of my bed, lost and low in spirits. The weight of planning and its related tasks lay heavy on my chest, yet I couldn't discard the apathy seizing my body. I let out so many long sighs when a maid knocked and entered that it alarmed her and sent her into a frenzy of endeavors to revive me.

It took eight days to set the arrangements to my satisfaction. The duration could have been shorter had it not been for a gamut of emotions, from low spirits to anger to trepidation, still possessing me. However, I was glad the preparations required me to avoid my fellow companions and saved me from the constant bursts of errands Lady Primeveire piled on my routine responsibilities.

On the morning of my departure, the ladies-in-waiting parted with tears. Had I not been wiser, I wouldn't have understood that they sobbed to soften me and to surrender me to their requests for procurement of items from faraway lands. I shed a few of my own—a farce, of course. It was to be my proof for later, when I could use my distraught state of mind as an excuse for evading their expectations. I had no intention of showering them with gifts. They didn't deserve my generosity.

As we set off from the Manor, I smothered the coachman's desire to cruise a gleam-flash. Father Bhumi had a mind of his own for generating and directing flashes of energy and light beneath the top layer of soil. Already swimming in anxiety, I had no patience to deal with the sporadic nature of the gleam-flash or dallying on the northern line of the official mainway, awaiting the current to whisk us off. The coachman wasn't pleased, but soothing him while worry wormed its way through my body was impossible.

After a month and a half in the confines of the coach, its body battered by God Vavajod three-quarters of the time and ours cramped and stiff for the whole duration, relief was got only during our brief stays at various manor houses. Horses were exchanged, repairs made, and supplies were refurnished. However, no amount of soap suds or local refreshments or socialization lightened my nerves, which, on the contrary, worsened as we neared Memora.

What if the witch refused Lady Primeveire's authority and declined to make another blanket? What repercussions would I suffer from my mistress? Challenging times would follow me. My lady would make more and more demands of me on sudden whims, and the others would find unending merriment in my suffering. And what about all the playacting I would have to produce to conform to the expectations of my role? The taste in my mouth turned sour.

Worse yet, what if my insistence enraged the witch and, in her agitation, she inflicted a curse on me? A lump formed in my throat. Either way, it would be an unpleasant ending. I wrung my hands until they were hot and ruddy.

If I kept these thoughts going, the situation could get quite complex and insurmountable—all before I set foot in Memora.

For the first time since my journey's beginning, I wanted others to back my appointed undertaking. Not the ladies-in-waiting, but plenty of reliable folks worked in the Manor. To face the witch with them would be an open demonstration of power. Although a crowd wouldn't affect her talent of sorcery, it could at least make her pause before wielding her curses. Unfortunately, I wasn't afforded such comfort.

Since no perfect scenarios existed, the best chance of success was staying on task and feigning confidence and authority. After all, I was talented in pretense.

Ranain

I huffed and plopped on the floor. My dead mother's chest held nothing but cobwebs. Although her belongings were long gone—perhaps the same day I had been forced to relinquish our home—the dried geraniums and juniper she used to keep pests from her clothes were untouched until now. Why would the villagers steal them when their abundance was undeniable in and around Memora? But they did, along with every other item in the house. To my amazement, the chest, though damaged, remained.

I shook my head. Why couldn't the villagers let our house alone? I couldn't afford to replace the lock each time.

A thud outside made me hurry to the entryway. The front door I had closed upon arrival was propped open, its broken lock swinging from the latch, and, outside, a group of men and women stood among the overgrown weeds and dead plants of the front garden. Their dark eyes and the earthy coloration of skin and hair did not differ from mine. Yet . . .

I swallowed.

"How long are you here for, witch?" the tavern owner's wife said in her gravelly voice.

The word they flung around with such casual hatred sent shudders through my body. It was like a yoke, leaden and crushing, placed on my neck as if I was some animal they wanted to keep in check, to corral me in a pen of isolation.

"I'm not a witch," I wanted to shout, but my courage failed me to use my name alongside the title they accorded me. Besides, my assertion was a bucket without water against the gales of the people's beliefs. No argument from me could convince them otherwise, so my thoughts withered inside me, as always.

"If you're planning to stay the night, you better not linger beyond tomorrow morning." The burly stonemason shifted his pickax from one shoulder to the other as he widened his stance. The point of his pickax was sharp. A nervousness crept up my legs as an old image flashed before me.

The tavern owner and the undertaker advancing to my house with a shovel and pitchfork . . . the pujari leading the group, his jaw determined and eyes glittering with hate, his hand that offered prayers and flowers dipped in honey and milk in the village temple gripped a sickle.

My chest felt as if pinned under an unwieldy material of stonemason's trade, and my breath struggled to function.

"I will leave soon," I said, trying to hide the strain in my voice.

A trail of people, some carrying children and others bearing makeshift weapons, approached the collapsed fence. Cold, hard eyes and scowls were prominent on the adults' faces, excitement and curiosity on the younger children's.

The uproar outside . . . my arms against my chest, breaths as frayed as my nerves, while I retreated to a corner of my house and pleaded in whispers, my appeals perceived only by me.

I sucked in a breath and dug my nails in the door frame. Why did I bother to come here without being summoned for their needs? Peering into the emptiness contained by the walls, I knew the reason. Memories of my mother and father lured me, a span when laughter and warmth and contentment and togetherness had abounded.

Fierce and smoky blazes of the torches bobbing up and down outside my window in cadence with cruel and slanderous insults . . . "witch" needling me like a hive's worth of bees . . .

"The witch is here," a woman shouted in a tone heavy with resentment and objection.

Her timbre painted the bare room in a new light of terror, which had befallen when the villagers had crowded around our house four years ago. My parents weren't alive to protect me. The same people to whom my mother and I had extended our generosity were raising their fists, cracking their knuckles, and throwing eggs and rubbish at our house.

Sweating and quivering as I crawled to the door, slamming it, locking it, and shoving the table against it in a last effort of self-preservation—all the while sure of the futility of my actions . . .

I looked away from the villagers and pressed my abdomen, willing the churning inside to subside, and sucked in a gulp of air to control my trembling breath. To think it would help was useless.

My twenty-one-year-old heart racing and my knees knocking . . . afraid of my skin and muscles melting over my bones, fearful of my ashes being lost in the charred remains of a burned down house.

My breath hitched.

"Are you in want of anything?"

I flinched. It was one of the two neighbors who had rescued me on that fateful day. She came closest to being called a friend, for I had no companions, no well-wishers, no secret-sharers. Had she suffered for the sympathy she extended me? Her goodness and her age reminded me of my mother. At the sight of her, the squeeze in my chest loosened.

"Are you and your family well?" I said.

She nodded.

"Call for me if you ever need me." I would never charge her if she ever desired my healing services.

As soon as she was gone, I threw one last glance at the cool interior and closed the door, sealing the horror that swept through me.

"I'm leaving now," I said to the others.

Upon receiving what the horde wished for, most of them went back to their chores, but a few tailed me, and they would not desert me until they saw me cross the gates of Memora. They were so predictable until they weren't.

The winding street led me through the section where the folks with no money or belongings to their name dawdled in hopes of work or pity or alms. I stalled. There were so many! Did no one think of them? How my mother's heart would have ached on seeing them.

"What is the meaning of stopping here every time you appear in the village unannounced?" a man following me said. "Don't look at them as customers for your ill work. They hardly have a coin in their name."

Harmful work? An urge to correct his false belief about my craft of healing swelled. I suppressed it.

We strolled along, adding children to our procession, their toy drums dragging behind their bodies by strings, the drumsticks striking with each turn of the wheels, beating in tune with the rhythmic march of my feet. That was, until we approached the communal ovens my family had owned.

"Stopping here to look at it won't make it yours again," the same man said.

I studied the large windows set in the brick walls with their chipping mortar with a twinge of jealousy. Each morning we'd opened those to air the heat of the ovens. And the roof . . . how many songs had it sung to me as the rain patted, pounded, pelted it in a storm while my mother had worked, and I'd helped? She hummed sweet melodies as she measured the flour on the table, created a well to receive the water I poured from a jug, gradually combined the dry and wet ingredients into a dough, which she then entrusted me to knead while she proceeded to the next one.

My childhood friend stepped out of the entrance, shielding her eyes from the morning sun. We'd lamented we weren't sisters at one time, but at present, she avoided my acknowledgment and sped inside.

Staring at my empty hands, I plodded toward the gates with the people in tow.

"Don't come back unless beckoned," a woman said.

When I looked at her, she mouthed, "Witch."

"Healer, not a witch."

Their label shouldn't bother me, but it did. In my mind, a witch dealt in dark arts, and I considered myself more of a medicine woman, curative versus injurious. She shrugged her shoulder, letting me know they didn't care and thought me the same.

No sooner had I exited the gates than the adults lost interest in me and withdrew, taking their children with them. My cottage squatted opposite to the entrance of Memora, separated by a wide thoroughfare, and that was where I headed.

A few days later, bathed in the morning sunlight, two girls bickered in hushed tones at my fence's entrance. They both froze when they saw me at my door.

"Do not go close to her, sister," the young girl of about six said. "She'll turn you into a toad, warts and all."

"How else am I to pay for her services?" The older girl walked along the path toward my steps while her sister stayed by the fence.

"Is your brother better now, Julisa?" I accepted her bread.

The loaf was warm and emitted a trace of ale. It stirred my mother's image: how she'd wiped her brow as she slid loaves of pastries and bread in and out of the ovens with her peel. Her bread was firm, uniform, and deep golden brown with no tears or bulges, unlike the pale one I held.

"Why are you addressing her by her first name?" the little one said.

"How is your brother now, Je Julisa?"

"He is sleeping and eating well now."

"You can call me Ranain," I said. "Or Je Ranain, if you prefer to be formal."

"I will tell mother you are talking sweetly with the *witch*. She will make you regret it."

Witch. The combination of those five letters and their intended implication, spoken with such hostility, hung between us. It prickled my skin.

A few years ago, their mother had lived under the open sky, alive wholly on account of mine. How passionately she had begged me for another person's share of bread and meat as I had gone on my daily errand of my mother's goodwill, promising to repay me twofold if she came to fortune. And now that she owned our communal ovens, she had forgotten her past. I didn't need her handouts, but the least she could do was not kindle dread and lies about me in her children.

"I'm a healer."

"You're an enchantress. Everyone knows it." The little one's passion raised my eyebrows. "You turn into a raven and fly into our village. Then you use your eyes and ears to spy on people. You steal and kill babies too."

How was I to fight these twisted perceptions, these untruths? Fed lies as soon as they understood words, these children would believe them until they grew up, until their souls left their bodies. Why wouldn't people accept these concoctions? To suppose otherwise was boring. Wasn't it more thrilling to know a person possessing wicked power? Conceive stories about their atrocities and whisper them to evoke a tingle of dread? Despite her uneasiness and misgivings, I perceived such fascination in the younger girl's lively eyes.

In my childhood, I, too, had deemed the witch—living in my cottage before me—captivating. Except she was a real sorceress, not some faint-hearted healer like me, and she could cast a curse with extraordinary skill. My mother had never taught me to loathe her despite a valid reason for apprehension. Neither had we ever called the genuine witch by any other name except her given: Richenda.

"Your hair is the proof," the little one said. "The color of crows. And you have black beady eyes, too."

"You *are* imaginative," I said, repressing a laugh. "My eyes and hair are dark brown, similar to you and your sister's."

The girl had infused her imagination into her hate. Lucky for her, she hadn't met Je Richenda, who had an aversion to mockery and offensive names and who had no patience to remain silent about her displeasure. Granted, Je Richenda had an unpleasant disposition and carried resentment with her everywhere like a soldier would a sword, but she was the opposite of hideous and cunning.

"I have to go," Julisa said.

How they all avoided meeting my eyes.

"If your brother needs further help, then come get me."

The sisters left my gate. They stayed far from the carriage stalled in the space between Memora and me, eyeing it suspiciously as they crossed the distance.

I considered the carriage for a few moments. The horses, whose muscles declared strength, power, and vigor beneath their lustrous coat of black, were taller than me, and the metal body they pulled was grand, the color of mature pine needles. One glance at the extravagance was enough to recognize the overlord's asset and to remind anyone of his large army and the power he wielded over the villages, hamlets, and cities dotting the landscape around and for miles away from Ashmere.

I hastened back into my cottage, intending to shut the door, but the coachman opened my gate and hurried along my path, calling me.

"What is—?" He recoiled halfway to me, his mouth and nose covered by the back of his hand. "It is the most odious—the vilest . . ." He withdrew to the gate, where he hurled the contents of his stomach.

I frowned.

"What is that offensive smell?" A rough voice spoke from the window of the carriage.

"Pigeon and berry stew," I said as I trudged to the spot where the coachman had hunched over and vomited. However, I could have mustered the courage to say, "Your coachman's vomit," but the imposing display of her position restrained me.

"I would not touch your stew even if I were writhing in pain from hunger." Her forehead, adorned with a string of pearls, was held high.

She had to be the lady-in-waiting to the Lady of Ashmere. Resentment for the lady and the family that she served overcame me.

"But do you even know what hunger is?" I asked, coming closer.

She raised her eyebrows, the same shade as the payment Julisa had handed me minutes ago before she narrowed her eyes at me. "Were you not taught how to behave in the presence of nobility?"

"Manners don't matter when people have banished you." The pressure on my chest reappeared, reawakening the memories of the horrendous day when a satisfying life had been cut short unexpectedly.

The lady-in-waiting furrowed her forehead at me. Their kind didn't encounter barefaced audacity—the sort I displayed—in their daily lives in Ashmere Manor, nor did they partake in impudent behavior while in the presence of someone of higher standing. But we weren't in Ashmere. We weren't even in Memora.

The coachman opened the door for me at the flick of her hand, exposing the velvet-lined interior of the warmest burgundy. She beckoned me. I balked at first. Then with one foot on the carriage step, I hoisted myself, slid into the seat opposite her, and waited as she shuffled to the corner farthest from me. I chuckled under my breath; her reaction reminded me of Julisa's sister.

"I am here because Her Ladyship wants more blankets," she said. With her facial features so soft, one assumed the same of her voice, but occasionally what one expected wasn't always what one got.

Had I heard her right? Had she said "blankets" and not "*a* blanket"? A surge of regret rose in me. If only I hadn't sent the first one out on the coach bound for Ashmere two years ago.

I wrung my hands and glanced at my cottage. An overgrown crab apple tree hid its right half, and ivy covered the left, while a flower, herb, and vegetable garden flanked the sides of the path leading to the door. It had been my home for the last four years.

"My blanket reached Ashmere Manor as intended."

"Yes," she said, not detecting my disappointment.

Two winters ago, I had gotten so ill from the whipping fury of Vavajod burrowing through the rotting mortar that I had gone mad with desperation. The gaps in the door were like a sieve, and the raw bites of the season had no trouble locating the holes. With a shivering, achy body and a rising fever, I plugged them with shawls, mats, and a sheet. Complete stoppage of the frostiness was impossible, and it drove me frantic. I was willing to do anything, even a rash act of initialing an association with the feared overlord's family, bringing their ugliness to the northern parts of Terra Two where we were safer from their grasp.

"Your Ladyship relishes the blanket," she said in her unpleasant voice. "Such a wonderful gift."

"Gift?" I snapped my head back at her.

"Yes, gift," she said.

But I hadn't sent it as a present; I couldn't afford to. It had been a cry for help. Now, if Her Ladyship was destitute, I would try to assist her. But she wasn't, was she? The proof was in the lady-in-waiting's presence and the carriage carrying her.

"Lady Primeveire sleeps through the night, no longer tossing in bed. And her mood and appetite have improved," the messenger said.

"Must be a relief for Her Ladyship," I wanted to retort, but—as much as I disliked admitting—I was pleased. It was one of the powerful spells from Je Richenda's books. It was self-taught, and it had worked! For a moment, I wanted to throw my arms around her and squeal, but I reined in and buried my elation. Our class differences made an embrace improper. Besides, the haughtiness she displayed was a trait I despised.

"Thank you for letting me know," I said, meaning it. After all, I wouldn't have known of the covering's virtue without her disclosure, considering the enchantment served only the intended.

"I'm sure such a deed is no feat for you," she said.

No feat? What about the extraordinary lengths I had gone through since its inception? And I hadn't even been confident of the spell's success then. A few chants uttered as I washed the woolen scraps, bits of fur, and linen pieces in the stream behind the cottage and as I dyed them and dried them. More muttered as I needled, threaded, knotted, and pieced them together.

"She wants one for her daughter, Lady Timothea, who recently lost her beau. And a new one for herself, since the one you sent has faded." She fiddled with her gold necklace.

"As presents?"

"Are you expecting a reward? How can you even dare?"

"I have no means of making blankets," I said, sagging back in the seat, hands falling to my sides.

"How did you make the previous one, then?"

Those strands of cloth I had used were discarded pieces; pieces I had stolen from the weaver's loom-house while I should have been sweeping, collecting the dust and lint in my casting pouch, singing cleansing spells with ringing bells, and burning sage and mugwort. Discovery of this offense could ban me entirely from the village, my parents' home, and access to the pleasant memories held within those walls.

"I have a solution," she said, looking bright. "We will ask the weaver to provide you with some yard goods."

"In exchange for what?"

"For nothing! Is not making the blankets for the pleasure of Her Lady-ship enough?" she said, her annoyance flaring, which she then corrected in the next breath.

I pressed my fist against my thigh and turned my body toward the door, fighting an urge to flee. The strain in my chest returned. I abhorred being cornered. A forever obligation to the weaver loomed before me. Worse was the risk of a lifetime of entrapment, of making gifts for the Ashmere ruling family. Who enjoyed being exploited?

"I have no threads or thimbles, and my needles are blunt and crooked. I need mordants to dye the cloth." The confines of the carriage became oppressive. "And what am I going to subsist on while I spend months making these blankets?" Tension had risen in my voice.

"Months? I thought you were a witch!"

I stopped my expression from turning hard and my tone tart. Respect for others, my mother's lessons, would not hold here. She reiterated the villagers' lies without seeking the truth. "I'm not a witch." I bit my tongue to prevent bitterness from tumbling out.

Her mouth slacked, and she darted her attention to the scenery outside her window.

"Very well, but why does the blanket take so long to make?"

"The plants for the dyes grow at different times of the year and—"

"Yes, yes. Her Ladyship remarked on how unusual and pleasing your colors were. In particular, the red and the pinks. She is weary of ordinary greens. And also, of the oranges and yellows and the browns." The lady-in-waiting fished in her beaded silk reticule and thrust copper pennies into my hand, careful in avoiding the touch of my skin. "What did you employ to get those colors?"

"Bloodroot and pokeberries—poisons," I wanted to hiss at her.

I scowled at the coins. Was this what the lady-in-waiting thought my exertions were worth? The villagers paid me better than what she shoved in my palm.

Bloodroot caused swelling in my nose and throat, heat in my face, and the awful feeling of my head being on the brink of bursting like mature seed pods ready to explode. I should have heeded the warning in the book, but the vivid scarlet sap was attractive, as enticing as confections to a child. Pokeberry wasn't better either; it raced my heart and made me want to do what the coachman did at my gate, except with such violence that my insides wanted to go the direction its contents did.

What had I been thinking using those plants the first time around? And to please Her Ladyship? One whose heart was as shrunk as a prune and purse strings as tight as the knots in my blankets? What schemes could I conceive to rid myself of the lady-in-waiting and her grand plans for me?

"The reds and pinks come from plants difficult to find." I wasn't good at deceit. Still, I lied.

"Try harder at foraging." She dropped another coin in the palm I had forgotten to retrieve in my state of irritability. It was a silver spard.

I gazed at her reticule, gauging its weight and guessing the number of requests it would allow her to make before either she yielded or I stormed out of the coach in a daring attempt of rudeness.

"Easier said than done." I crossed my arms.

"What can help? Do you need men to go scouting in the woods behind your cottage? Villagers cannot refuse Lady Primeveire's command."

A thread of alarm twisted around my heart, making me speechless. Those villagers would seize my parents' home if such an incident came to pass. I took in my cottage through the door; leaky though it was, it was a warm-hearted shelter. And it was mine.

"Well, then, how can we solve this dilemma?" she said, her persistence as resolute as my mother's charity had been bottomless.

To say I understood my folly and learned my lesson was not an over-statement. But it was too late to undo the decision I had breathed life into two years ago, and in its consequence, the lady-in-waiting was before me.

I had no inkling of joining her in her pursuit of a solution, but who could in their right mind refuse the high nobility's desires, even if it came through one of their representatives? Their requests were demands in disguise, capable of destroying one's life if not submitted to, even in far-off lands like Memora.

"I will use other colors," I said.

"Reds and pinks." The lady-in-waiting signaled for me to open my fist and added six more coins to the collection in my palm. "Solely employ those two colors."

What trouble had I stirred! Why was she pushing me to bargain?

Haggling with the villagers was one thing, but with a member of the high-ranking noblewoman's household, the behavior resembled folding too far over the edge of the well. Being myself and expressing concern, however restrained, was a dare enough. And the deal she offered—the headache, the retching, the troubled breathing—was the worst. My mother and I had helped Je Richenda during childbirth, after the death of her child, and later when her health failed. But who would care for me if I sickened from the poisons?

Misleading her made me squirm, but I had to forestall her from making additional perilous appeals. "Those plants are not from this region. The find was pure luck the first time around."

The lady gave a quick inhale and exhale and plopped the whole reticule in my hand.

Great Goddesses, the woman was relentless!

Hinder, hinder, I told myself as an urgency bubbled. "Isn't sleep more valuable to Her Ladyship?"

"Why can I not choose both sleep and pleasurable colors?"

I glanced at my cottage again. So many nights I spent stooped over a book, studying a new remedy as the drafts flickered the candlelight. The old roof couldn't bar them from whistling their way through and winding around my rickety furniture and through my baskets and drying herbs. I took comfort in the thoughts of my belongings and habits.

I straightened my back and adjusted my clothing. "Those reds are from poisonous plants. One blanket was bad enough. Multiple will weaken or kill me. Then, no magic will be left in me to weave a sleeping spell into the blanket. So, which matters more to Her Ladyship—color or sleep?"

The lady-in-waiting's eyes widened, and her fair skin paled. Was it my directness or the subject? Or was it the prospect of delivering unpleasant news to her lady and expecting retribution for her part-failed errand?

Not wanting to give her a chance to recover and object, I continued, "Red sumac berries give a most remarkable reddish-purple. When paired with some yellows and rich purples, it will be glorious. And I could add some brilliant pinks if I can find some wild raspberries or wild cherries."

"Sleep is important," she said, somewhat recovered but distracted by a stalled couple cowering at the village gate. "Does the weaver in the village have crimson goods? Or maybe someone else dyes the same shade of red? Perhaps I can have someone stitch the blankets. All you would have to do is charm them."

I sighed.

If the villagers came for my services, headstrong in their approach and desires, I refused to indulge. Except this wasn't an ordinary subject, and I could not behave as per my choice.

At any rate, my pigeon stew had charred by now, and I would have to fish if I wanted something besides plain bread. The thought of the labor made me close my eyes and draw a breath. The coins jingled as I moved my hands. Or I could buy something. Except they'd suspect my sudden wealth. Would they refuse to sell me a rabbit or beans?

"My magic won't work on fabrics not infused with love and care." I was unsure of this, but one matter was clear from my short years of being a healer: healing couldn't happen if love and care weren't stirred in the mixture. Besides, I didn't want the weaver or others to be forced to bestow their good grace.

"You are so disagreeable." She furrowed her brow. "I can see why you live at the edge of Memora."

My wavering focus sharpened on her. I didn't need her painted lips or her lavish dousing of rose perfume. I didn't care for her silk attire, her wavy tresses, or for the weight she dropped in my hand.

"My stew is inedible by now." I half-rose without permission. "The pot will need a good scour to make it usable again, and the cottage would need a thorough airing out to rid the stench from my bedding and clothing and books. Imagine if Her Ladyship's blankets were in there, halfway put together, on my worktable next to my hearth . . ."

The lady-in-waiting blanched. Her forehead was beaded with sweat.

"We wouldn't want that now, would we?" I got out of the carriage.

She called after me, her voice faltering. "What kind of witch are you? Can't you use incantations or magic to make the blanket?"

"And what kind of lady-in-waiting are *you*?" I wheeled. "Led by a so-called *witch* and her persuasion, instead of threatening me with imprisonment or beheading?"

"So you won't strike me in a state of fury?"

"I would never—" My mouth fell open.

Who had they conferred with? How far did the falsehood of my being a sorceress extend? Not that I had dealt with the overlord's proxies before, but her restrained mannerisms and the fact that she wasn't doling out threats at every turn in our conversation had to have a reason. And fear had to be it.

"Are you frightened of me?"

"Of course not!" She gulped her saliva.

"You think I can change the weather or fail harvests? That I can curse and unleash horrible diseases on people or their livestock? That I can fly on a broom, cackling at the cruel jests I administer? You are far too mild-mannered with me. Is it because you don't want to infuriate me, lest I unleash a hex on you and the nobility?" My voice had increased in force and loudness by the time I finished.

"You . . . you should be the one watching your back," she said in an unconvincing tone.

I hurried to my cottage, red-faced. As soon as I stepped in, the acrid odor assailed my face, singeing my nostrils and watering my eyes. I poured ash over the embers to deaden the fire, then wrapped a towel on the handle and brought the scorched pot outside. The congealed mess, hardened and blistered and fastened to the bottom, made me wither.

While I fretted with the problem at hand, the lady-in-waiting crept behind me and gave me a scare. A cry loosened out of my throat. Thereupon, she recoiled as if I was about to bewitch her.

A swift apology wasn't a sufficient balm. Her eyes bulged, unblinking, as though an entire forest behind my cottage had come alive and was about to swallow her whole. She swayed, and when she sank to the ground, she curled on her knees. Her moaning and blubbering made no sense.

I nipped my lip and looked about. What had overcome the lady-in-waiting? No such scenario had arisen before, nor been described in the books, nor during the few times I had apprenticed under the neighboring hamlet's healer.

I tore to the water bucket inside the cottage and sprinkled a glass of it on her.

Did the coachman know his passenger had exited the coach? If he burst upon us and saw her lying next to my steps, wallowing in wretchedness, he would assume I had used the dark arts. How would he know devilry was not in my nature? No amount of convincing would abate his suspicion.

I would be bound and hauled to Ashmere. What would be next after reaching there? Dungeons? Being strung? Maybe impalement? I stilled. They thought I was a witch. They would burn me—delivering me to the fate that had almost touched me once. Good Goddesses!

I redoubled my effort with the water and splashed the whole bucket on her head. Next, I tore fistfuls of herbs from the bed, crushed them with fervency, and shoved them in the collar of her dress, behind her ear, in her hair, and between her fingers curled against her face. Then I heaped them under her nose, praying the pungency of lemon balm, rosemary, garlic, and sage revived her. Why had I not replenished my smelling salts? I jostled her with rude ferocity until sweat lined my skin and my limbs were tired, feeling as heavy as a sopping woolen blanket.

Much to my relief, the lady-in-waiting recovered. She looked about, dazed, before she regained her awareness. I took her by the elbow and led her to the bench in the crab apple tree's shade. She covered her face with trembling hands, sobbing in a way that unsettled and puzzled me. I sat by her until she was somewhat restored.

"You don't appear to be short on patience," she said in a shaky voice when she realized my presence. The conventional requirements of her upper-class social behavior had vanished, her arrogance purged. "And you have hurled no evil at me."

She removed the herbs from her ear and her dress, and holding them against her nose, she breathed as if she'd been deprived of air. She tugged at the pale roses of the wild vine running up the tree and drew in their sweet, spicy scent.

"I don't practice malicious magic. I can't cause sudden illnesses and deaths or turn crystal-clear rivers into muck. Nor can I change people into toads or birds or mules or cats."

"I beg you to close your door and windows and put the pot as far away as possible," she said in the same shaky tone.

I gave her a blank look.

"Please."

"I will honor your request, but I expect an explanation."

She hesitated. When I didn't move, she said, "Do I have to?"

"You have made many demands of me today," I said.

She studied the dense blackthorn hedges hemming the side of my cottage and gave such a slight nod I almost missed it. I closed the house openings, dropped the pot in the stream behind the house, and joined her on the bench. Her composure returned, but she held more flowers and herbs close to her nose than when I had left her.

"Promise me you won't share this with anyone," the lady-in-waiting whispered.

I searched for the coachman. He was atop the coach in his front cabin, far enough for his interested ears to eavesdrop. Upon my assurance, she related the accident from her childhood. Her gaze became distant, lost in another world, and her voice ebbed and trembled like it had lost its strength. Her eyes went misty, and she hunched over, her arms crossed against her stomach in a protective huddle. It was a harrowing misfortune.

It reminded me of mine. My breaths became uneven, and my chest tightened at the memory of the swarm of venom-spewing people with weapons and torches surrounding my home as I cowered in a corner, helpless, afraid for my life, the cold walls my sole support. Except, however trying my experience was, her losses were more profound, her details more gruesome. The notion of fire and burned bodies always weakened my courage, but it was just that—an idea, a fear. It wasn't so for her.

She was here on a mission to get blankets for her mistress's peaceful nights, but how was her sleep? By her reaction to the odor of my charred stew, her ordeal haunted her often. And if she was keeping this a secret, how forlorn was her existence? And I thought *my* occasional bouts of profound loneliness and painful longings were unusual.

So absorbed were we with her story that, at the end, when she moved, I realized I held the messenger's hand, without permission, a taboo for any local peasantry. I unclenched in a hurry, and her eyes widened as if she'd forgotten I sat beside her. The gloom in her face turned to apprehension. She realized in reporting her ordeal, she had inadvertently revealed her secret.

"You gave me your word not to divulge what I shared. You can presume the predicament I would be in if . . ."

"I will keep my pledge," I said. "But how were you able to hold a position in the Manor when you were not born a noblewoman?"

She wavered, then considered me, possibly weighing the consequences of trusting a stranger, a so-called witch in particular.

"Does Her Ladyship know?" I said.

"Hope not." She glanced at the coachman anxiously. "In my youth, I was obsessed with securing the position I hold now. No amount of coaxing by anybody dampened my will. To realize my dream, I found and signed an agreement with a former lady-in-waiting. One who was forced by the noble household to give up her position. But that trifle didn't matter to me. I was elated when I got selected for Lady Primeveire. It was the pinnacle of my existence. I had feigned my upbringing and passed." She swallowed. "Little did I realize then that I had to maintain the veil of deceit for years. That, too, among people who delighted at my every misstep, my every flaw. And I lost my family and friends."

I was no stranger to friendlessness, and I was well acquainted with isolation.

"I'm Ranain," I said.

"I'm Anum." Regrets of her life lingered in her voice.

"Why did you come after me?"

"I wanted to convince you about the blankets," she said, creasing her forehead. "I *cannot* go back to Lady Primeveire without them. Whatever colors you decide are fine, as long as you agree to make them for me."

"My relationship with the villagers is strained."

"Why? Is it the reason you live outside Memora?" To my surprise, she grabbed my hands, the crushed flowers emitting a fresh round of fragrance.

"Because despite the villagers' displeasure, my mother and I helped Je Richenda—the witch who owned this cottage before me. Then after my mother's death, when the benefits they received from her evaporated, people became intolerant of our friendship. And when Je Richenda died and bequeathed me her property, they doomed me to the same destiny as hers."

The dark experience left my mind's recesses for the first time and escaped into the daylight in the shape of words. Each sentence was laden with misery, but a sense of relief washed over me by the time I finished, the stirred agony dissolved, and I felt cleansed. Even being condemned and driven out at a young age, I realized I had endured the loneliness and pain with grace my mother would appreciate.

Anum wiped the wetness off her cheeks, the flowers falling by our feet.

"Why would you ever get involved with her? Weren't you afraid of witchcraft?"

"Witches are people too," I said. "Besides, I was never taught to fear Je Richenda."

My heart ached for my mother. She had perished too early, despite Je Richenda's efforts.

Anum's eyes were wide and unblinking. "Were you never tempted by black magic?"

"I burned Je Richenda's books on sorcery. I don't want them in my cottage nor anywhere in Memora."

We let our realities sink between us. We studied each other's faces.

"I was afraid of you," Anum said.

"Seeing the overlord's carriage in front of one's dwelling isn't a soothing sight, either."

She chuckled. "I've been shut in the Manor for so long I'd forgotten how foreboding the Overlord Drilll is to regular folks and the power he represents."

I nodded.

"Will you convince the weaver?" she said.

"The weaver will refuse to loan me anything. He won't believe me about your request even if I pay him." I extended her reticule to her; she refused. "The villagers tolerate me for one reason. The doctor's history is cloudy, just like his right eye. The people accepted his self-professed medicinal skills when he appeared in Memora because they didn't want to rely on Je Richenda. Now they are trapped in a cycle of bloodletting and amputations and vapors, no matter the type of illness. So when sicknesses arise or when people need to be rid of evil spirits, villagers come calling, especially for their children's lives. My herbs and potions and chants and charms are their sole saviors. Yet they would shun me in a heartbeat if their resentment overtook their needs. They could even expel me out of my cottage and burn it."

Anum blinked slowly. "It's worse than the isolation I feel in the Manor. This is exile."

"But I'm not trapped like you."

With a grim twist to her mouth, she said, "Neither is tolerable."

We sat in silence for some time, shoulders touching, slightly leaning on each other.

"Then I will visit him and pay him to do so." She dragged out a second reticule of ivory silk, embellished with colorful embroidery, from her long sleeves. "I will also mention about my return to mark the progress of the blankets." She paused and smiled. "And to meet *you*."

My face expressed surprise, which amused her.

What was this soothing and accepting connection between us?

"A moment." I hurried indoors to the cupboard of glass bottles of varied shapes and contents and gathered a cobalt and an amber vial. Then, as I wiped them off with my skirt, I roamed among my flowers and herbs to remove the house's malodor before returning to the bench.

"What is this?" Anum studied the cobalt container I placed in her hand.

"Something to remember me by."

She hesitated, but when she unsealed it, a surprise of sweet William, thyme, and a hint of wild raspberries released in the air. One whiff, and she gasped, coloring her cheeks.

"Perfume." She emitted a short bark of laughter. "It is so—delicate, yet—perplexing."

Nobody became giddy with happiness on my property or in my presence. I felt lifted, experienced a sensation of floating as the dandelion tops did on a breeze, and I couldn't help but like her.

"If my lady smells this, she might want it too." Anum's smile tottered, alluding to the predicament that had befallen the blanket.

I had an aversion to obligations. They were traps and reminded me too much of crowds and pitchforks and torches and narrow spaces.

"But does she need to know it was from you?" she said.

I drew my eyebrows together. "What will you say?"

"That I bought it from a peddler hawking his wares off the side of the road. I'll share it with her if she demands it. Otherwise, the perfume will be mine to enjoy. Others will be envious. I would enjoy seeing regret on their faces for forgoing an opportunity to travel. To procure such an item."

I handed her the amber vial, and she offered me a questioning glance.

"This one's for sleep," I said. "For your nightmares."

Her face broke into the gentlest, most amicable look when she understood. It reminded me so much of my mother's dimples and her crooked smile. I bowed, but she pulled me close and bound me with a long hug.

"Your cottage is so lovely," she said upon releasing me.

"Isn't it?"

"Except for the stew you were cooking." Mischief lurked in her lips.

It felt good to laugh.

After a glance in the coachman's direction, she embraced me a second time before saying goodbye and returning to her coach. The driver secured her door, took my directions regarding the weaver, and returned to his seat.

"Many thanks to you." She poked her head out of the window as the coachman turned the carriage. "I'll write to you."

I waved her farewell and stood regarding the carriage until the kicked-up dust marred its clarity. Then I looked back and considered my cottage nestled in its thriving garden. The sun cast its brilliance through the trees. Birds twittered and darted about from the thorny hedges, and the breezes swayed the flower heads while smuggling their fragrances to my nose. Amid all this, there in the shade underneath the crab apple tree was the bench, of old chipped stone, its filigreed curved legs a home to moss, solely used as a place to rest my garden basket while I plucked and picked what the ground gave me. But today, on that bench, I had received a bounty like never before: a well-wisher . . . ally . . . no, a friend.

Anum

I was gripped by euphoria. The pressure I placed on the weaver in the overlord's name irritated him, and he hesitated at the thought of helping Ranain, but he buckled at the sight of a fistful of gold, silver, and copper. The villagers, assembled at his place in curious disapproval, also sounded no protests as I parted.

With my tasks accomplished, the coachman and I returned to the road. Again, I forbade him to use the mainway, although the reason differed from before. Could not the journey I had regarded as punishment be a boon instead, a continuation of respite from ridicule and an escape from the pretense that had been stifling me of late? To waste such a rare opportunity of freedom was stupid. I was almost of a mind to dally my journey home. What was an extra month or two at one of the manor houses en route when the entire journey, back and forth, cost half to two-thirds of a year anyway? It would not do, though. Not if I were to continue as Lady Primeveire's lady-in-waiting.

Instead, I made resolutions: I would rejoice in the beauty of the lands, associate with their people when possible, and savor the meals prepared by people other than Ashmere cooks. If the coachman disapproved, so be it because he was of no consequence. I could feed him persuasive reasons, as I would to those in Ashmere Manor.

The surrounding lands of the mountains flitted by. The wildflowers and the shrubbery dotting the wild ditches and the steep slopes of the road, narrow and serpentine, and the sun playing with me through the thickets of trees stirred hints of my younger years. It shook memories of my playmates.

Ranain. The name rolled so smooth on my tongue. Reminded me of rain, soft and refreshing, quenching the thirst of the parched land. Opening the cobalt vial, I took a sniff and was instantly transported to her garden, her kindness, and her cool hands in mine.

What a dolt I had been for looking for a friend in the wrong places! Even a bigger one for believing the falsehoods circulating in the Manor about the witch.

"Halt!" I banged on the roof of the coach when we had reached the foothill.

"We shouldn't be stopping here," the coachman said, stepping down as I exited, his forehead furrowed. "We have far to ride."

The air was fresh and moving. The fields, stretching for miles, were more vibrant than the most expensive emeralds in Lady Primeveire's jewelry box. Above, a large flock of birds swirled back and forth.

"Starlings," I said, delighted.

When they fluttered away, several other birds descended; they flitted about, looking for seeds and insects, singing elaborate calls. I had been familiar with those melodious songs and known the plumage of those birds. Except it had been years since I'd heard or seen them, so it took me longer to recall their name.

"Larks," I said.

"If you are fond of lark pies, I could stop at the closest inn for you," the coachman said.

Was there ever a time when the nobility and their faithful exalted an item's or a being's quality for anything else besides its immediate benefit?

"It's unnecessary." I climbed back into the coach, and we continued our journey.

A decade had passed since I entered Ashmere Manor, a time during which I was expected to forget my desires in the nobility's service. A decade! They said there was no need to venture outside since everything was provided within its boundaries. I saw now the prison as it was and what measures were implemented to keep it so. My confinement had made me, I realized in shame, forget the small joys that made life meaningful. The memories had seeped out so quietly, leaving an ignorant and a depthless person behind.

How keen had I been to shed my old self and quick to transform into the title I coveted? My mother's objections had fallen on deaf ears. After the fire, we had been destitute. Yet I'd persisted in my misplaced devotion and loyalty to the nobility, and my yearning for belonging in their household had multiplied as time passed.

Where had my dreams gotten me? I shook my head. Outside of Manor life, I didn't know where to go or who else to be. A gust of wind, heavy with the scent of freshly cut summer straw, blew in through the window. The flitting green outside and the memory of the birds restored my mood. All was not lost. A portion of my old self was still alive. Ranain would help me find it, unbury it.

B ack at the Manor, the ladies-in-waiting flocked my ride even before my feet touched the ground. They cheered and peeked inside the carriage's body for gifts, then sulked when I reminded them of my distress at departure, of my ignorance of their expectation. Their disappointment soon turned envious the moment they sniffed me. Greener still, when Lady Primeveire lauded my efforts and bravery and relieved me of my responsibilities for two days to recover. They glanced sidelong at my sun-blessed complexion, displeased with the similarity to theirs, and begrudged my uplifted mood.

They didn't matter anymore. And Lady Primeveire was no longer the center of my life. I'd tasted the outer world now and realized it was way bigger than the Manor grounds, richer than the Manor life, no matter how tightly the royalty cinched my world. Best of all, I had a tether to this outside world: a compassionate heart whose name was Ranain.

And she was my friend.

HELLO READER

I hope you enjoyed reading this book. I appreciate you picking it up.

If you liked my stories and want to avoid missing out, I suggest you head to my website nikipatelauthor.com and sign up to receive my emails. There's no charge or obligation. And you can unsubscribe anytime you want.

Sign up, and I'll make sure you hear about every new book when it is ready to be published.

Also, when you're at nikipatelauthor.com, don't hesitate to send a comment. I would love to hear from you.

ABOUT THE AUTHOR

Weary of averting her grandfather's constant persuasion and frustrated by her inaction, Niki Patel picked up the pen one night and emptied her brain on paper.

By the time she wondered if she wanted to sustain the habit, she was elbow deep in tales. Her stories are one part love of nature, one measure of gardening and food, the nostalgia of her life in India, and the rest, a twisted imagination of her mind.

She resides in the United States.